"F

A Novel by CJ Lines

hadesgate

publications

Published by:
Hadesgate Publications
PO Box 167
Selby
YO8 4WP
Email: hadesgate@hotmail.co.uk
www.hadesgate.co.uk

"Filth Kiss"

A Novel by CJ Lines

First published November 2007

CJ Lines asserts the moral rights to be identified as the author of this work.

Mailings to: CJ Lines
               c/o Hadesgate Publications
               PO Box 167
               Selby
               North Yorkshire
               YO8 4WP
               www.hadesgate.co.uk
               www.hadesgateforums.co.uk

This novel is entirely a work of fiction. The names, characters and incidents portrayed in it are the work of the author's imagination. Any resemblance to actual persons, living or dead, events or localities is entirely coincidental.

ISBN 978-0-9550314-5-8

Cover design by Keith J Burton at The Mouse Department
www.themousedepartment.co.uk

Prepared and printed by:
York Publishing Services Ltd
64 Hallfield Road
Layerthorpe
York
YO31 7ZQ

Tel: 01904 431213   Website: www.yps-publishing.co.uk

For Brenda and Robert Reid with my love and
thanks for everything.

In loving memory of John Arthur Lines (1946 – 1995).

ACKNOWLEDGEMENTS

I'll keep it brief as no one ever reads these things unless they're mentioned, but my thanks to the following people are sincere enough for me to want to write them down. They have all contributed, one way or another, to my writing this atrocity you hold in your hands. I hope they don't wind up in court or sectioned as a result.

First off, thanks to Paula and Ray at Hadesgate and to Garry Charles for their enthusiastic support and their unflinching devotion to the horror genre.

A massive thank you to my editor Janie Chan, for her excellent copy work on the "Filth Kiss" manuscript and her continual support. Her impeccable taste in food and sake is also a constant education.

My huge, genuine thanks also to Oliver Redfern, without whom, "Filth Kiss" would never have begun; to Suzi Brent for the advice, the years of friendship and writer's block camaraderie; to Krys Plucinsky, for enduring my shit while I wrote this; to Tina Williams and to Steven and Jez Thurgood for reading the horrible unproofed drafts; to Stephen Shoard and David Gardner, for being my fanboys in Nottingham; to David Ryder, for getting the ball rolling and because I promised I'd thank him someday for it; and to Joel Taylor, for always being there when it really counts.

My thanks also must go to Guy N. Smith and Mary Flanagan for inspiration and support way beyond the call of duty (and probably more than either of them realise).

Finally, my thanks and all my love to Sarah Dobbs, for bringing the Forest to life (and for "Filth Kiss: The Photo Album"!).

That's quite enough of me. Hope you all enjoy the book.

C.

PROLOGUE: SWEET KATIE

"For nothing, I called you my friend, for nothing.
No, you have pillaged and broken me …
You have poisoned my life!
Now I moan because
you have beslavered my lover's sweet lips
with the filth of your kisses
You will not escape your fate.
The future will know you, as you are."
- Catullus

He wrapped the dead girl's clothes into a bundle around the rock and threw them in the river. They floated clumsily on the surface then moved away with the feeble current. He had lost track of the time after midnight struck and had no idea how long was left until they would notice she was gone. *Sweet Katie Brown.* Yes he loved her in his own way. A kind of pure, protective love a father might have for his daughter. Not his sons though.

That's why he had to help her. Because he loved her. He had already reminded himself of this love's strength when he had been cradling the rock in his arms, wondering whether or not he could force himself to bring it crashing down onto her sweet skull, obliterating her eight doomed years of existence once and for all.

It was for her own good.

He held out his hands in front of him and inspected them. The blood was drying and had turned to a rusty brown crust on his skin. He snorted to himself and recalled *'Macbeth'* in his mind, before a rustle in the bushes brought him back to the task at hand. He had to dispose of the body before sunrise. Before they came looking.

Overhead, a birdsong drifted through the nocturnal stillness and he knew that more time than he had estimated. The sun was beginning to rise above the tips of the trees. It must've been in the small hours of this last cursed night, when he had sat with Katie by the riverbank, trying to justify to her what he had to do.

"Why are we here?" she had asked him, her voice a picture of gaily innocent curiosity, as she splashed at the water with her feet.

"Because you're beautiful and I love you," he had replied solemnly.

1

"You're silly," she giggled.

Was it hours or only minutes after this when he had been wiping, with disgust, fragments of her brain from his fingertips and picking the tiniest shards of bone out of his nails?

He looked at the corpse laid out on the grass that almost shimmered behind him in the moonlight, and realised he had to move her. He needed to take her somewhere remote and burn her. It was paramount that she could neither be discovered nor identified. He would not risk them finding her and taking her away.

He heard the rustle again in the bushes and then the shouting started.

"There's something over here! A car!" he heard a young man's voice yell. It seemed amplified by the silence surrounding it and startled him into a state of heightened alertness.

He ran towards the corpse and scooped her up in his arms, stumbling off down-river towards where he knew there was a small alcove of bushes in which he would be able to hide.

It's too late. The voice inside his head echoed, brutally reminding him that they'd found his car. They already knew that she was gone and that he was here. They would know what he had done too. They had known it was coming all along. He was a fool to think that he could deceive them just because he had felt love at long last, after all these years.

Before he could reach the alcove, he heard the shouting become increasingly cacophonous behind him. He dared not look back. He knew that they had seen him and he broke into a run, clutching the dead girl to his chest in desperation. *How many of them were there?*

He felt a small stone collide with the back of his head like a bullet and the shock sent him tumbling towards the grass. The corpse flew from his arms as he floundered and tried to ease the pain of his landing. He fell flat on the ground, face to face with the pulpy remains of Katie's shattered skull.

He screamed. He screamed with such force and ferocity that it scared him into screaming again. He screamed for his life, he screamed for sweet Katie Brown's life, for the lives of the mob rushing towards him, their angry footsteps sounding like a herd of elephants hurtling down the bank, and he screamed for all the others; the ones he couldn't help.

"Look at this," he heard one of the men exclaim, as the footsteps behind him stopped. He dared not lift his head to look at them. "The fuckin' bastard! Look what he did to her!"

He felt a sharp, searing ache as the man's boot connected with his side. Soon one boot turned into many and the forceful kicks came from all angles, showering his body in a hailstorm of pain. He tried to move his arms up to cover his head, but they were kicked out of the way. The verbal abuse continued to hurl at him, an endless flood of hateful obscenities. *"Don't they know? Don't they know that I loved her?"* He started to cry tears of love, of pain, of fury, and of failure.

After awhile the kicking ceased, the jeers died down to a few whispered grunts and a woman's voice ordered him to turn around.

Slowly, through the agony of the bruises already screaming to burst through his skin and the sting of freshly opened cuts, he turned to face her. He had known she was going to arrive sooner or later. Her grey, spindly hair blew in the wind and looked like snakes, hissing and writhing in the moonlight. She fixed him with a glare, those ancient eyes of hers projecting hatred from within their tired, wrinkled lids.

"Is it over?" he asked weakly, coughing up a thick stream of blood and phlegm.

"Don't be so pathetic. You know full well it's only just begun," she replied. Rage washed over her features, turning her face into a mask of horror as she began to chant in the language of the angels. He knew all too well what was coming next and began to pray. To whom or to what, he was unsure. He just fired desperate words into thin air, hoping for some salvation to arrive from anywhere.

The corpse of sweet Katie Brown sprang to life beside him, flicking stray shards of brain and blood into the air as it sat bolt upright, straddled his chest, and wrapped its tiny hands around his neck.

He made no effort to break free and heard the sound of her melodic, innocent laughter echoing through his ears. Her puckered, bloody mouth, filled with broken teeth and bile moved towards his. He smelt the foetid stench of putrefaction and would have vomited had the corpse of sweet Katie Brown not then locked lips with his and, in her vile unearthly kiss, sucked the life from him.

PART ONE: PETER AND JEFFREY

The Dreams and Desires of Fleas
A Trap is Set

"Ambition, cruelty, avarice, revenge, are all founded on lust." – The Marquis de Sade

I

The office was hot, airless and had Jeff Davies wilting at his desk. Although the Holborn streets outside the HBG Telecoms building were ravaged by savage autumn winds and a vicious chill, the new air conditioning system ensured the employees felt like they were being slow roasted all day. It made Jeff sleepy, lazy, and dry-mouthed. He stared at the numbers on the screen until they became impenetrable hieroglyphics. His eyes were misty and stinging again and he realised he would just have to go tell his manager he couldn't hack today any longer.

Jeff stood up and walked across the open-plan room, heading towards the large glass door, currently obscured by black plastic blinds, behind which the office of Chris Merricks lay. He knocked on the glass and turned the handle, letting himself in meekly.

"Hi Chris," he began, consciously avoiding eye contact.

"Jeff. Hey there," replied Merricks amiably. "How's things with the Lynch installation? I hear you ran into some problems with getting the cable supplies."

Jeff was taken aback and racked his brain for a few seconds to even remember this particular job, despite having dealt with it for the past week or two off and on. "Err, oh yeah. We got that sorted, I think. Penery set up an alternate supplier and we managed to expedite it over to Galloway before they even noticed there was anything missing."

"Good work." Merricks clicked his fingers and winked. His eyes then shot back to the paperwork he was going through on his desk.

"Thanks, but, um, that's not why I came to see you. I

just, um…" Jeff struggled with the words, feeling a vague sense of professional embarrassment at showing weakness in front of Merricks. "I just want to ask if I can go home for the rest of the day. My Father died last night."

There was an uncomfortable silence. Merricks shifted a handful of post-it notes from one side of his desk to the other and began clicking his retractable pen in and out. "Of course, take the day off," he eventually said, smiling and standing up. "Take the rest of the week if you like, all you need."

"Thanks, Chris," Jeff replied. "I appreciate it. I just, I just… don't think I can do this right now."

Merricks approached Jeff, put an awkward hand on his shoulder and patted it. "I'll have Rob take over the Lynch stuff for now. Is there anything else you've got on that needs covering?"

"Not really, I'll hand things over to Rob now if you want, just to let him know what's what and stuff. Most of it's stored in the Accounts directory. He knows what to do."

"Sure, thanks Jeff. I'm sorry about your father. Were you close?"

Another uncomfortable silence.

"Not really," replied Jeff, as Merricks' hand finally slipped from his shoulder and returned to clicking at the pen. "We haven't seen each other for a long while. He lives up North."

"Oh yeah, that's where you're from isn't it? Up there?"

Jeff thought it was amazing how, in London, you could work fairly closely with someone for several years on a professional level and barely even recall so much as rudimentary knowledge about their personal background. With Merricks shut behind his glass door all day, the only real times they communicated were if there was a crisis that needed dealing with or in the weekly team meetings, where little beyond corporate strategy was discussed. Any other fleeting occasions where they had spoken were those uncomfortable encounters in the office canteen where they had been forced to share a table on days when it was too full to be able to sit alone.

Nonetheless Jeff answered the question, secretly hoping the social niceties would be brief and merciful. "Yeah, I was born just outside of Gloucester. My dad still liv... lived there."

"I'm sorry. I don't mean to pry."

"It's ok. I'd... I'd just better go tell Rob what he needs to do."

"Sure, sure. Thanks. If you need anything else, just let me know. I'll see you next week ok?"

"Yeah. Thanks, Chris."

"Any time. You take care of yourself. Look after your mum too."

Jeff decided to let that one pass without comment. It would've been impolite and awkward to point out to Merricks that his mother was also dead and had been for seventeen years. Instead, he just smiled, nodded and left the room, heading back towards the four-way split desk where his colleague Rob Parker was about to have his workload doubled for the week.

"Got some bad news, mate," began Jeff, smiling sheepishly.

* * *

Jeff left the office and walked across Red Lion Square. The wind bit at him and seemed even harsher than usual now that it contrasted against the sweltering artificial heat of the office. The trees in the square were predominantly bare and the odd cluster of dead leaves brushed across his feet. A pair of young, unwashed men sat on one of the benches, knocking back cans of Tennants Super. Upon seeing them,

Jeff knew exactly what he needed to get himself through today. A drink.

The atmosphere in the Square Pig this Tuesday afternoon was quite lively, all things considered. A few City bankers in sharp light-coloured suits still lingered from their long lunch hours, sipping bottled beers. A couple of students gravitated around the bar, laughing and joking over pints of lager. Some tourists with rucksacks sat at a large table, chattering loudly, curiously absent of drinks. Elderly men sat nursing murky pints in corner booths, chewing on their fingernails, rolling cigarettes or drawing aimless circles in puddles of split ale. Anything to keep their hands moving, make themselves look busy, hide the fact that this was all they had to do today. Or any other day, most likely.

Jeff shuddered, as he often did looking at these men. He feared more than anything that he may some day become one. Aside from his job as HBG Europe's Communications Executive, a presentable position with a tidy salary and decent enough prospects for a man of thirty-five years old, there were few other things to cling to in his life. He had no partner, few friends to speak of and now even his family was diminishing before his very eyes. He sometimes felt as though he was slowly just drifting away from the rest of civilisation and that he would soon wither away and become one of these dried-up husks in the corner booth, slowly drinking himself to death... He wondered what their stories were.

Get a grip, you wanker.

Jeff composed himself and ordered a pint of Stella. He settled himself down at a table and began to dwell on the death of his father.

Jenny had called him at home this morning from Broadoak at 6am to break the news. She sounded distraught and yet somehow detached. "Dad's dead," was all she said at first, over and over again. Eventually he managed to coax more information from her and the more she spoke, the calmer she began to sound, even though the feeling that she could've been talking to a complete stranger instead of her own brother grew strong, as the call went on.

It transpired that Guy Davies, at sixty-two, had drowned in the river Severn, on the outskirts of Broadoak whilst hiking before dawn. A local man, engaged in the very same pursuit, had the misfortune of discovering the body, just floating on the Severn. Jeff's eyes began to mist over a little. What a horrible, undignified end to a life. *But a life of what?* Jeff barely even knew his father. His parents had divorced when he was too young to even remember and his mother had raised him and his brother in North London, whilst Jenny and their father had remained in Gloucestershire. The family had been split in two and this rift never healed. Although Jeff visited each Christmas and kept in occasional touch over the phone, he still saw his father and sister more as strangely distant acquaintances than his own flesh and blood. Now, sat in the grizzly half-light of the autumn afternoon, in a bland London pub, he wondered how things might've turned out had he stayed with the father he barely knew. Maybe life would've turned out different. Maybe better?

Oh dear God... Shut UP!

Again, Jeff caught himself wavering towards self-pity; teetering above the edge of the chasm of misery he felt forever poised at these days. He tried dwelling on the positive side. At least things hadn't turned out as badly for him as they had for his poor brother...

Ah, yes, poor Peter. Poor, twisted Peter.

Jeff knew that Jenny would not have made the effort to call Peter with the news. She would have left it down to him. She'd made it quite clear she never wanted any contact with him again after what had happened before. The grubby payphone at the bar was pockmarked with cigarette burns

11

and looked as though it hadn't been used for awhile. Jeff walked over to it, found 10p and prepared for the worst as he dialled his brother's number.

II

The copper beech trees swayed in the breeze as Sarah Hobson stared out from her spot on the raised streets of the town. Even the spectacular view of the Forest of Dean from across the Severn had become humdrum to her. She had been sat at the bus stop for fifteen minutes and had given up hope of getting out of Broadoak tonight and going into Gloucester for a gig. She took her jumper from where she'd tied it around her waist and slipped it on above her washed-out yellow school blouse. It was getting cold.

John Piper, a lad from the village, was walking up the road and Sarah decided she would rather avoid conversation with him if possible. He was beginning to discover his hormones and, for some peculiar reason, seemed fixated with her, even if the rest of the school seemed to ignore her and treat her like some kind of unwelcome stain on their comfortable little landscape. She actually much preferred this silent treatment to the persistent attentions that John Piper lavished on her. She went out of her way to blend into the background, into the darkness, dying her hair jet-black and always wearing her school jumper and long skirt, trying to show as little of her pale, almost translucent, skin as possible. The other girls in her year, who were now at the age where they were shortening their own skirts with DIY dressmaking, mocked her for her refusal to adhere to their styles. In her mind she reviled them for their vapid ignorance and lack of understanding. She refused to rise to their constant baiting and spent much of her break time at school locked in the girls toilets, reading books.

"Hey Sarah, wait up!" John Piper yelped as she began walking off hurriedly in the opposite direction.

"Sorry, I have to go see someone," replied Sarah, without looking back.

"Hey, I just wanna talk to you, is that so bad?" he asked, his voice taking on a whining, nasal property that made her skin crawl. "Why can't we just talk?"

"Please, just go somewhere else, ok?" she snapped, exhaustedly. "I'm not in the mood for your shite today. It's too cold, the bus has gone missing and I've had a bollocks day, alright?"

Walking towards the banks of the river, Sarah didn't bother to look back. She knew that, as annoying and pointless as John Piper may be, at least he knew where to draw the line. He would not follow her. Very few people came walking to the river when the sun was going down. A fine cloud of mist was rising up the banks and the tips of the trees were arching across the last fading glimmers of sunlight. It would be probably only half an hour more before the forest was plunged into darkness. The small village of Broadoak had already switched on its streetlights, but they could scarcely be seen from where Sarah now sat, shoeless and dipping her feet into the sludgy water of the Severn.

She opened her school rucksack and pulled out a small polythene bag of marijuana and a pack of rolling papers hidden between her notepad and science book. Squinting to see against the rapidly diminishing light, Sarah made up a joint as deftly as she could and lit it, taking in the first deep inhalation of the sweet, numbing herb with aplomb. She closed her eyes and felt for a second as if her whole world existed only in the few feet of grass and water surrounding her.

About a minute later, her bubble was burst by the feeling of something sticky and bulbous floating down river, colliding with her left foot. She opened her eyes and looked downwards at the murky river, blackish-brown in the impending evening gloom. Propped up against her foot was a bloodied, ragged-looking human hand, its gnarled, dead fingers locked into a talon-like curl. Sarah leapt up and brushed down the lower half of her leg with her hands, sweeping off the mud and weeds of the river.

"What is this shite all about then?" she murmured to thin air, taking another long drag of her joint. She bent down and picked up the hand. It was heavier than she had expected and covered with sticky river scum. She attempted to uncurl one of the fingers, only to have it snap off with a dull cracking sound. She laughed gloomily and noticed a silver ring stuck to the severed digit. Discarding the hand in a bush, Sarah began to prise the ring off. It seemed to be quite ornate; small bands of silver patterned to look like two intertwining serpents. The type of thing that she'd probably end up spending at least £20 on, if she bought it at Gloucester market. She finally wrenched the ring off and it came free with a weak crunching sound. She slipped it into the pocket of her trousers and decided to make a move towards home, lest anyone see her.

The sight of the hand floating in the water had not shocked her. She was used to finding the remains of animals in the forest and had spent enough time in her father's butchers shop to not find dead flesh particularly repugnant any more. Her only concern was that she might be blamed for whatever had happened here, so fleeing the scene seemed like the smartest idea.

It was a short walk back up the bank and towards the village but by the time she arrived back on Monmouth Street the sky was black and appeared to be preparing itself for a storm. The clouds were writhing around a sickly-looking quarter-moon and Sarah felt the buzz from the drugs begin to wear away as she approached the terraced frontage of number three. She fumbled in her rucksack for a set of keys and let herself into the house.

Her father was slumped on the front room sofa watching a documentary on television, which appeared to be about wild cats hunting one another in Africa. He was cheering as one of them ripped a chunk of flesh from the other's back, and only turned around when the fight was over and the narrator's voice began talking above topographical images of the continent.

"Oh, 'ello Sarah, how were school today?" he asked, flashing a smile of troublesome yellow teeth.

"Same old," she replied in an uninterested tone and began making for the stairs.

"Why don't you stay down here and watch some telly?" he said, his voice seemingly taking on a similarly nasal whine to John Piper's earlier that evening. "I've had a bloody terrible day. Freezer's still bosted. I can't get anything to keep and I can't find a bloke to come fix it until Tuesday."

"I have to do my homework," she lied. She simply wasn't in the mood to listen right now, nor watch any more tedious wildlife programmes.

Her Dad's smile faded a little and he turned back to the TV. "Alright, well, see you for dinner then. I've made rabbit stew, your old favourite."

"Yeah, see you later."

"Don't play your music too loud Sarah, your Mum's gone to bed."

"Sure."

Sarah walked up the stairs quietly, past the stair lift, and headed to her room. Although her mother's room was right next door to it, she felt a sufficient degree of privacy in her bedroom to be able to relax. Every visible centimetre of wall was covered with posters of heavy metal musicians and counter-culture heroes. Above her bed hung a gigantic red and black swastika flag with a bright white skull painted in the middle. She had bought this not out of affiliation for extreme right wing politics; indeed she had no care for politics of any description. She had bought it partially to shock her parents, but mostly because its striking primary colours, looking down on her from the ceiling made for fantastic visuals whilst stoned.

Sarah had fitted a lock to her bedroom some months ago when she first started smoking at home. She now bolted it closed as she slung her bag on the bed, removed her school uniform and changed into an Alice Cooper t-shirt and black baggy trousers. She lay on the bed, headphones blasting out heavy metal as she smoked another joint and stared up at the bright white skull on the ceiling.

A good twenty minutes passed before Sarah remembered the silver ring she had stolen earlier. Springing up from the bed and detaching her headphones, she removed it from her school trousers' pocket and went to the bathroom to clean it up. When properly washed, the ring looked even more eye-catching. It was indeed a pair of silver serpents with small rubies for eyes. The ring slid almost perfectly onto Sarah's finger and she smiled at herself in the mirror.

"Hiss! Hiss!" she spat at her reflection, raising her hands and flashing the ring. "I'm a sssssnake!"

She chuckled to herself and headed downstairs upon hearing her father call her for dinner.

III

Peter Davies limped nervously into the Square Pig and loosened the top buttons on his grey Barbour jacket. He had been caught in a rain shower on the way over and his thick blond hair had flopped across his face, obscuring his vision momentarily. He flicked it away with his fingers and walked over to a small circular table where Jeff was sat. It had been over a year since they had last met face to face.

"Hello," he said self-consciously, clutching his arms tightly to himself. "C-c-c-can I get you a pint?"

"Hi Peter, sure," replied Jeff, smiling. He had loosened his tie in a slovenly manner and looked distinctly more weatherworn than the last time Peter had seen him, some six months ago. Jeff's wiry blond hair was beginning to recede a little and the bags around his deep blue eyes were making them appear a weaker shade than before. More grey than blue. His shirt had clearly not been ironed for a day or two and his smile seemed tired and forced. Although there was only two years between them, Jeff now looked at least five or ten Peter's senior.

Peter walked to the bar, where some students were gathered and merrily sipping trendy bottled drinks or Babycham. He ordered a pint and eyed up one of the girls without much discretion. She was probably no older than 16 or 17, a little old for his private tastes if he were honest, but still young and pretty enough to make his groin tingle as he looked her up and down. She had long brown hair, tied up in a ponytail and a short denim skirt. Her skin was lightly tanned and perfectly complimented the strapless khaki top she wore, which left little to Peter's imagination. *She's young enough to be your daughter,* he thought to himself and it was precisely this revelation that caused the erection to spring up beneath his trousers. He wanted to pull it out there and then – to show it to her – but he fought against the urge with well-practiced restraint. After all, he had had those long, agonising twelve months in that cell to rehearse self-control. The slightest violation of his parole and he would have at least another thirty-six of them to regret it.

It was safe to just look though. Every man looks. Peter found it strange that as a teenager, he never believed he could get away with staring. He would steal a fleeting glance then turn away, as though he were above it, yet secretly wishing his gaze could linger longer. Of course, back then he had been so self-conscious. With his limp and his speech impediment, he had been unpopular enough with the opposite sex at school as it was, and didn't need lechery to be added to his list of flaws. Now, at thirty-three, he realised he had no chance with young girls anyway; he was old enough to be completely off their radar. They didn't even notice him eyeing them up, on trains, in pubs, anywhere. He may as well have just been the shadows or the dust in the air.

He began feeling old and melancholy and was relieved when the barman returned with two pints. Peter took them over to the table and sat down opposite his brother.

"I know, I look like shit," he said. He always thought it best to pre-empt put-downs and say them before the other person had chance. "But I'm doing o-k-k."

"Actually, you look a lot better than last time I saw you," replied Jeff.

"The prison slacks did nothing for my c-c-c-c-complexion." Peter tried to make a joke out of it; pretending it didn't hurt, as ever.

"Heh. Yeah." Jeff sipped nervously at his beer.

Peter grinned. "You c-c-ccould've c-come see me after I got out, you know."

"I know. But, well," Jeff trailed off and paused for a few

19

seconds. "We've been through this."

"It doesn't feel right still?"

"No, it doesn't. I'll be honest, I only called you tonight because of what happened to Dad."

An uncomfortable silence fell. Small talk never came easily to either brother, but after Peter's conviction, conversation at all between them had become an immense struggle.

"The funeral's Saturday in Broadoak," Jeff said eventually. "Jenny said I could come up, tomorrow, stay for the a few nights. You can catch a lift if you're up for it."

"Thanks. I am."

"I don't think Jenny will let you stay though. You'll need to find somewhere else."

"No problem. I don't think I'd let me stay either." That self-mocking grin again.

"I'm leaving London at about midday, if you want to pack some stuff together and meet me at my place."

"Same place?"

"Yeah."

The brothers sat in silence, both sipping their pints quicker than was entirely comfortable. Peter scanned the bar and lingered again on the denim-clad buttocks of the student girl at the bar. Jeff discretely blew a silent belch out of the side of his mouth. He was clearly a little drunk already and Peter wondered how long he'd been sat in the pub.

"The dozy fucker drowned in the bloody Severn," said Jeff, snorting.

"Yeah, you said."

"What kind of a way to go is that?"

"I thought Dad c-c-c-could swim, is the weirdest thing."

"He could. Jen said he knocked his head or something on the way in."

"He fell in?"

"Yeah."

"Jesus."

"I know you didn't get on with him these last few years, but still…"

Peter lifted his glass and finished Jeff's sentence with a toast – "…here's to Dad."

"To Dad," said Jeff and they clinked glasses. "May he rest in peace."

IV

The girl writhed naked atop the wooden coffin in the dank of the funeral parlour's basement. Her body was wrapped around the box in unearthly contortions. Her amber eyes glowed in the darkness as she rubbed herself with her fingers and took long, deep inhalations of the stench of death. The air was foetid and thick with decay, excrement and formaldehyde.

She convulsed with pleasure and hissed loudly, her hair cascading down her face as her head jolted back and forth. The door opened, shedding light into the chamber. It was the old woman. Her voice was throaty and harsh. Her crooked frame stood silhouetted in the doorway, hunched over her walking stick, as if ready to fall over.

"Enjoy the old fool's flesh while you can, dear," she said to the girl. "They're burying him on Saturday."

The girl leaped off the coffin and slithered across the floor towards the crone. She used her long, spindly fingers to brush a tangled mass of auburn curls out of her face and stared up, those yellow eyes shining with eagerness and raw sexuality. The crone raised her walking stick and presented its ornamental tip to the girl who licked its silver serpent design up and down. Her forked, inhuman tongue flicked across it with rapid movements.

"Have your feed tonight," the crone continued. "Tomorrow you must find a substitute for the bairn."

With that, the girl removed the silver serpent from her mouth and slithered back to the coffin. Raising the lid, she looked inside and greeted the grey, battered remains of Guy Davies with a vicious grin. She ran her fingers along the corpse's torso and slowly manoeuvred herself into the coffin, until she was straddling the chest. She took each of its arms in hers and raised them upwards, to reveal only one of the hands was still present. Shrieking with laughter, she dropped the handless arm back into the coffin and pulled on the other one, rocking back and forth atop the body, until eventually the second hand snapped free in hers.

The arm flopped back onto the corpse with a dull thud. The girl took the hand and kissed it sensuously, flickering her forked tongue along each finger in turn. Carefully she took the dead hand and placed it between her legs, forcing it inside herself. First one finger at a time, until eventually she was lubricated enough for the whole appendage. With a push it disappeared wholly into her, making an almost comical popping sound, and she threw her hair back, screaming now with ecstacy.

The crone looked on as the outlines of the hand, now brought back to hideous life, moved through the girl's body, making its mark on her flesh. The lumps of knuckle and finger stretched the skin, pushed it outwards, moulded its shape into red raw protrusions that literally crawled through the girl. She shrieked again as the outline of five fingers appeared, spreading out of her left breast, struggling to move upwards, trying to break out from their fleshly jail.

As the girl rocked herself on the corpse's torso, the hand moved upwards through her throat, its outline now clearer than ever, pushing to burst free from within her flesh. With a gurgling, rattling sound, she opened her mouth wide to scream with exquisite pleasure. The hand erupted from out of her throat, its soaked red fingers wriggling wildly, and leapt out from between her lips, landing on the floor beside the coffin. She collapsed atop the corpse and kissed its bruised, bloodied face passionately. The hand lay on the stone surface of the basement, now lifeless once more.

The old crone smiled to herself and left the room.

The snake-like girl pressed her naked flesh against the cold, debased remains of Guy Davies and fell into a blissful sleep, purring into dead ears.

23

V

The drive from London to Broadoak passed slowly, but without incident. Peter had arrived at Jeff's house on time and the journey had been predominantly motorways, the M4 and M5. The first two hours of the journey were spent in near-silence, the lack of conversation compensated for by a zany lunchtime show on Radio One that had both brothers chuckling discretely. This helped lighten the mood a little and, by the time they were approaching Gloucestershire, the DJ was wrapping up the show with a new song by a popular British guitar band.

"That was 'Make My Kitchen Warm' by the Omniscient Nostrums. Blinding stuff there, especially for Chris Thomson and the boys from the HBG warehouse in Galloway who rang us to wish J.T. a happy birthday today. Keep it real, Joel!"

Jeff laughed and shook his head. "Ha, I can't get away from them."

"You still work there then? At HBG?"

"Yeah. Just kind of stuck in it now."

"You like it?"

"Not really. It's just the same old shit each day really. But it pays well I guess."

"Yeah."

Jeff left the motorway and followed the signs towards Monmouth.

"I've got a job now," mentioned Peter.

"Oh yeah?"

"Yeah, it's just at the loc-cal chip shop, but it's c-c-cool. I just go there four nights a week but it pays o-k-k and it's better than nothing. It was hard to get anything after I got out. Oddly enough, a degree and a few years experience c-c-counts for fuc-ck all when you've got a rec-c-ord."

"Yeah…" Jeff trailed off without passing comment. It made him uneasy to talk about Peter's time in jail. He still found it hard to think of his brother, sat next to him now all harmless and calm, to be a registered sex offender. As horrible as it made him feel to play the 'ignorance is bliss' card, he just tried his best not to think about it at all. It was the only way he could share a car with the man.

The talking stopped again and they both continued listening to the radio until they approached the grey and rusty-brown sign that read 'BROADOAK' in black, unwelcoming letters. The tops of the copper beech trees in the nearby Forest of Dean loomed before them and the hilly greenish-brown landscape of rural Gloucestershire in all its autumnal splendour took both brothers' breath away slightly, as ever. They rounded the corner of a steep B road and looked down upon their hometown. Even though the weather was murky and bland, wholly unremarkable for this time of year, it still looked lovely from here, all ancient buildings and bushy undergrowth, leading up to the subtle majesty of the river Severn.

"Heh, makes a change from London, eh?" remarked Jeff.

"Bit different, yeah."

"It's weird, I always think of Christmas, whenever I come down this road."

Peter smiled. "Me too. I guess that's c-c-cos we only ever c-came here then. Did we ever even visit once in the summer?"

"I don't think so, no. It's weird. I never really thought of it like that. Still, it's a nice feeling. Heh. I wonder if old Taverner's brewed his mulled wine already."

"Heh, yeah, that stuff was nice. C-C-Christ. Only in Broadoak would you get a bloke with a name like Taverner actually owning a pub."

"Nah, that's not true, could happen anywhere. Just in London it'd be called something tacky like Taverner's Tavern."

"Taverner's Top Totty Tavern."

"Taverner's Tremendous Top Totty Tavern."

"Taverner's Tremendously Trendy Top Totty Tavern."

"Taverner's Tremendously Trendy Top Totty Tavern For Toffs."

They both burst out laughing.

"Hahaha. God, London's so bloody shite sometimes."

"Hey, I like the tack. I think I'd go c-c-crazy if I had to live in Broadoak all my life."

They drove towards their father's house on Nailsworth Road, smiling and at ease, an effect that Broadoak subconsciously had on them. Jeff knew the roads intimately, as though it'd only been yesterday since he had last visited.

"You want me to drop you off at the hotel?" he asked Peter, as they slowed down outside the house.

"It's ok-k, I'll walk-k there from here. It's only five minutes."

"I don't think Jenny wants to see you right now. I'll maybe try to talk to her in time for the funeral, but she was pretty angry when I told her I was bringing you up here."

"I'll get a move on then before she sees me. Cheers for the lift."

"Don't mention it. Want to meet up later at the pub for something to eat?"

"Sure."

"Cool. See you at eight, ok? The Old Crown."

"O-k-k."

Peter removed his travel bag from the back seat of the car and began walking towards the Bull's Head Inn, where he had made a reservation. Jeff, meanwhile, walked up the drive to his father's house and rang the doorbell.

26

Jennifer came to the door, smoking a cigarette. She looked quite different to when Jeff had last seen her, the previous December. Her peroxide blonde hair looked faded and thin. There were bags under her blue eyes and her lips bore the marks of being frequently bitten. For the first time ever, Jeff could honestly say that his sister looked her age. She was no longer the sweet and perky teenage girl he had known in his childhood. She was a woman in her forties, with a definitive demeanour of the defeated hovering around her.

He felt a pang of guilt for having barely spoken to her in the past twelve months and reached out to hug her. She returned the embrace weakly, but suddenly tightened and began sobbing heavily into his shoulder.

"Hey Jenny, it's ok," he said, rubbing her shoulders. "Let's get indoors. I'll put a brew on."

They walked inside the house and Jeff was instantly hit by the familiar smell of his family home. The smell of stale tobacco from his father's pipe; of the lavender air freshener spray that Jenny had always been so fond of; of her cooking, rich with lard and slightly burnt pastry. She sat down on the brown, busily patterned sofa – a relic from a bygone decade – while her brother went into the kitchen to make tea.

"Heh, I used your old favourite mug," he said, handing her a beaten-up cup with 'JENNIFER' written on it in faded red bubble letters. Jeff had remembered her using this mug to always take hot cocoa up to bed with her every Christmas Eve.

She sniffled and took it gratefully. "Thanks. I'm sorry. I've been really trying to hold it in, but it's hard."

"About Dad, yeah? It was a shock."

"It's not just Dad. It's just, like, how did my life come to this? You know?"

"Heh. Yeah. I often wonder that myself. About me, that is."

27

"I don't know how I'm going to cope now. My life seemed to be just, well, looking after him. Playing wifey, almost."

"Well, I'll stay as long as I can. My boss is pretty cool, he's given me the time off to come up here for the funeral and he said I could take as long off as I needed to."

"Thank you. I might not be here that long myself, mind you. I think I might have to consider maybe leaving Broadoak after the funeral. I'm toying with selling the house."

"Woah, seriously? Where would you go?"

"I don't know. Anywhere but here." She looked away shyly at this point.

"Why so sudden? What's wrong with Broadoak? I thought you were always pretty settled here? With Dad?"

"Maybe that's just it," she said, raising her head back up to face Jeff. "Maybe I just don't want to be here without him. I don't know. You'll see for yourself. The town's changed." A flicker of vague, unidentifiable menace seemed to flicker in her eye as she said this.

"Changed, how so?" Jeff was asking more out of desire to keep the conversation flowing than genuine interest. He didn't suspect Broadoak would ever change too dramatically.

"I can't... I can't..." she began to sob again. "I'm sorry. I'm just not... I'm..."

"Hey, Jenny, don't worry. Look, can I get you anything? Do anything? I'm here to help, ok? I know it's hard." He smiled benevolently.

"You've no idea, Jeff. You hardly even knew him. I thought I did. I really thought I did. I just... I don't know any more what I knew. What I know."

"Shhh," he whispered, putting his teacup on the mantle and sitting next to her on the couch.

"Oh Jeff, I've not even been eating lately. I can't even

face food. I just feel so sick and scared all the time."

"Are you sure you don't want me to get you something from the store? I'm going up the pub to eat later with Peter, but…"

She stopped sobbing. "So he came then?"

"Yeah."

"Bastard."

"You should maybe go easy on him. He's pretty screwed up in the head but I dunno. It's his dad too. You can't deny him the right to say goodbye properly."

"Don't you dare tell me what I can and can't do!" she snapped, rising to her feet.

"Woah, hang about. I'm just saying…"

She made a high-pitched noise of frustration, cutting him off yet clearly holding back on what she wanted to say.

"What?" he begged, exasperated.

"Oh forget it. I'll speak to you later. Or tomorrow. Whenever. Enjoy the pub, I'm sure it'll be an education."

She stormed upstairs, leaving Jeff sat in the living room alone with his travel bag and tea for company. He shook his head and exhaled loudly. Jenny had always been the most outwardly emotional member of the family and he was used to similarly unexpected arguments flaring up without warning. He never quite knew where she was, what she was thinking. It was as if, a lot of the time, she wasn't even too certain herself. He glanced at the clock and saw it was 4pm. Getting up, he drained his cup of tea and decided to go for a walk around the town, in order to see just how much it had apparently changed.

VI

"Change? My arse," he muttered to the wind.

The old town was almost exactly how Jeff remembered it. The row of little shops along the High Street had been there for as long as he could remember. Piper's The Newsagent. Hobson Butchers. Flowers by Ethyl. Yer Tiz. These relics of his early childhood were interspersed by more well-known chain stores. Woolworths, Budgens, John Menzies. The town library stood imposingly at the end of the High Street, a large Gothic building that dominated the view. Scattered solicitors offices and estate agents peppered the side-roads leading off from the high street. Jeff saw his old favourite sweet shop, Hundreds And Thousands.

He walked inside and the little doorbell let off a delicate ring.

"Jeffrey Davies!" shrieked the portly old lady behind the counter, her long grey hair flapping wildly as she ran out to embrace him. "My goodness!"

"Afternoon, Mrs Deering," said Jeff, smiling uncontrollably. The shop always made him feel good. Row upon row of old fashioned sweets in plastic tubs adorned the walls. Candy canes hung from the ceiling. Glass jars behind the counter. It reminded him of being young.

"I had a feeling you would be up this way," mused Mrs Deering warmly.

"Yeah, I'm here for the funeral."

"Yes. Terrible business, terrible business with your father."

"Yes."

"It's probably best not to dwell on these things, dear. I knew him for so long. I was very surprised. I can't imagine how it must be for you." She put a hand on his shoulder.

"Well, yes, it was a surprise for all of us."

"Of course. Terrible business, terrible business. So how are things in London anyway, dear?"

"Oh, you know, same old, same old." Jeff began to stalk around the shop, armed with a plastic scoop and a paper bag, collecting a stash of his old favourites. Sherbert lemons, vanilla fudge, Trebor mints, fruit bon-bons.

"Are you married yet, dear?"

Jeff laughed. "No, Mrs Deering, not yet."

"Handsome man like you, for shame!"

"Well, maybe one day, I don't know."

"Don't you worry now, your time will come. You're a good boy, you are. Not like that brother of yours."

"Peter came up with me this morning."

Mrs Deering looked at him imploringly. "He's evil, that one, dear. You should steer clear of him."

"He's... got his problems."

"Well, I suppose it's no surprise now, dear. Terrible business."

Mrs Deering took the bulging bag of sweets from Jeff and weighed them out. "That'll be fifty-five pence, dear."

Jeff was paying, when he heard the ring of the bell again and turned around. Sarah Hobson had walked in, rucksack slung carelessly over her shoulder, school shirt dangling out of the bottom of her bottle green jumper. It took Jeff a second or two to recognise her. He hadn't seen her for probably three or four years. Her mousy brown hair was now dyed jet-black and her pudgy, awkward face had formed into a sleeker, more feline shape. It was amazing how much a physical appearance could change in those key pubescent years between nine and fourteen. She was almost a young woman now.

"Hey, Sarah Hobson?" he asked, raising an eyebrow at her.

"Yeah?"

"Remember me?"

"Yeah. You're that guy's son aren't you? The dead one?"

"Sarah!" snapped Mrs Deering.

"Whatever."

"It's ok," Jeff said, calmly.

"Cool." Sarah was already uninterested in the conversation. She picked up a bag and took an overflowing scoopful of chocolate raisins from one of the tubs.

Jeff shrugged and smiled at Mrs Deering. "Oh well, see you soon anyway."

"Yes, dear. Do have a lovely day."

Jeff walked out back onto the high street and noticed it was beginning to rain. Tiny spatters of rainwater were peppering the pavement, so he decided to grab a Gloucestershire Tribune from Piper's and head straight to the pub.

The Old Crown was as traditional an English pub as you could hope to find. Long mahogany benches and ornate glass windows. Old cask pumps and little glass bowls of crisps adorned the short bar that was shrouded a little behind the thick cloud of tobacco smoke that drifted through the stale, damp air. Taverner stood behind the bar, puffing gently on his pipe. He cut a massive figure of a man, bulky, tall and wide, his bulldog features hidden behind a wiry grey beard. Jeff had no memory of him ever looking any older or younger. Always just the same.

"Hey lad," said Taverner, nodding to Jeff.

"Hi Taverner," replied Jeff. "How's things?"

"Oh you know, the usual, mind. Not a lot changes 'round here, does it? Sorry to hear about your father, lad. Awful business, mind."

"Thanks."

"First drink's on the house, what'll be? You deserve it, lad, after what you must've been through."

"Hmm, do you have any mulled wine yet?"

32

"Oh, I'll have to check. I think Mrs Taverner may have brewed up a fresh batch, mind."

Taverner opened a creaky wooden door and disappeared to the back of the pub, while Jeff scanned the pub for familiar faces, without much luck. It was still too early for most people to be here. At this point in time, there were only three other customers. Two of them were unrecognised men in Barbour coats and mud caked Wellington boots. They were sat in the corner and deeply engaged in what seemed to be a very private, almost whispered conversation, trying their best to ignore Jeff.

In the other corner of the room sat Bridget Drake by herself. She was drinking a glass of something pale and smiling, but her eyes had a faraway look that was entirely keeping in character. Her brown curly hair zig-zagged down her nose and she blew it back up again and giggled. Jeff had vague memories of Bridget in infant school. She was a hyperactive child and was eventually moved away to a special school outside of Broadoak. Jeff had only occasionally seen her since then, but he kept a wide berth, aware that she had mental difficulties and never really sure what to say to her or how to approach her. She met his gaze briefly and bit her lip. For a woman in her thirties, she still managed to look no older than seventeen or so. Perhaps it was part of her arrested development or maybe just a naturally girlish demeanour that was impossible to be rid of. Either way, it made Jeff uneasy.

At that moment, Taverner returned with a mug of steaming mulled wine. The fruity aroma immediately hit Jeff's nostrils and he felt himself beginning to relax again.

"That's the fella!" he exclaimed.

"Glad to be of service, lad, enjoy!"

Jeff tipped his mug weakly in Bridget's direction then went to sit at the furthest table away from her as he could find, unfolding his newspaper hurriedly and pretending to read as intensely as he could. It was only as he turned to the second page that the headline grabbed him and he stared slack-jawed at the page in mute horror.

"Is this true!?" he yelled at Taverner, springing up from his seat and waving the page of the newspaper at the unsuspecting landlord.

"You... You didn't know?"

"No! Jenny just said he drowned."

"Well he did. They fished his body out the Severn, din't they?"

"But what's all this about a missing girl? How the Hell does that fit in?"

"Come on, Jeff, sit down." Taverner cast his eyes around the remainder of the clientele, who were all now watching this suddenly very loud conversation.

The landlord walked around the bar to Jeff and guided him back to the table. "I don't even know if I should be the one to tell you this," he began, in a soft tone of voice, "but some funny things were 'appening with your father, mind."

"Like what?"

"He was hanging around this young lass..."

"Hanging around?"

"Well, he was always buying her toys, taking her down the park, getting her sweets. It were a bit queer if you ask me, mind. You know what people are like, we all talked a bit. Wondered what it was all about. But it seemed 'armless enough I guess. With 'indsight, you know? Her parents didn't mind."

"What...? Who was she?"

"Her name's Katie Brown. I guess 'e just took a liking to 'er. She were a nice kid, mind."

"And now she's... disappeared?"

"Two nights ago, aye. He was the last person to be seen with 'er. He picked 'er up to take 'er out to the park on the night he died."

"But this thing in the paper says…"

"I told you, people were talking, lad. I'd steer well clear if I were you – a lot of folk have got their own ideas about what your dad was doing with Katie Brown, mind."

"Oh Jesus…" Jeff covered his mouth in horror.

"It doesn't help, all that stuff what happened with your brother. They're saying it must run in the family. You know what they're like 'round 'ere."

Jeff felt a wave of nausea flood over him. The acrid mix of sherbert lemons from earlier and the taste of the mulled wine felt like stinging bile in the back of his throat, threatening to rise up again.

"I'm sorry, mate, I have to go," he croaked to Taverner, his face becoming pale.

"Jeff? Lad?" he heard the landlord call, but he was already long out of the door, newspaper grasped in his sweating hands.

The weather had well and truly broken and rain was pouring down heavily outside the Old Crown. Jeff used the newspaper as a makeshift umbrella but it soon became like papier maché and quite useless. Big drops of water splashed into his eyes and as he wiped them away he nearly bumped into little Johnny Piper, who was running in the opposite direction.

"Sorry!"

When he reached Nailsworth Road, he furiously hammered on the door of his father's house, waiting for Jenny to appear once more. She came to the door, looking tired and bleary-eyed. He had visibly woken her from an early evening catnap.

"Jeff? Where... what?"

"Why the fuck didn't you tell me?" he exploded, pushing past her into the house.

"What?"

"About Dad! I had to read it in the fucking newspaper!"

"Oh."

"Oh? OH?" He mocked her tone of voice. "God, I feel like such a fucking fool. I can't believe you didn't tell me this before I even came up. Did it just slip your mind that the whole bloody county of Gloucestershire thinks Dad's a kiddie fiddler and just maybe a murderer too?"

Jenny burst into tears, weeping loudly and covering her face with her hands. Jeff glowered at her, his chest rising and falling visibly with each frustrated breath.

"I... I can't even bear to think about it, Jeff."

She looked so vulnerable and afraid that his anger began to dissolve. He approached her, flung his arms around her and squeezed tightly.

"Christ, Jenny," he said, himself choking back tears. "What the fuck happened to this family? What the fuck happened?"

VII

John Piper's day had been awful. First and foremost there had been the embarrassing slanging match with Andy Murphy at lunch about John's crush on Sarah Hobson; a point of contention to his reputation, that all his friends ribbed him about. He blushed now, even thinking about it. Secondly, he had received a poor mark for an English project he had deemed to be quite reasonable, and to cap it off, his parents had somehow managed to lock him out of the house and vanish somewhere. The fact that it was now raining heavily, just added insult to injury.

John was thinking about Sarah again as he walked down Nailsworth Road and made towards the bank of the river Severn to seek shelter in the bushes. He didn't even know why he liked her so much. They had barely exchanged more than ten words at school and even less outside of it, but she fascinated him nonetheless. A lot of the other girls at school had asked him out and he'd even gone with a few of them, but he could never get Sarah out of his mind. He was growing an erection as he walked, just from thinking about her. Her long, black hair. Her fiery brown eyes and lush pale skin...

He eventually reached the riverbank and sat down under a sheltering beech tree that stood towering above an alcove of brambles and briars. He liked it here. He knew Sarah sometimes liked to come here and being here made him feel closer to her, even though he'd never dare be here at the same time, for fear of upsetting her. He was just sat there, thinking, when he heard the voice behind him.

"Hi Johnny," it said, in a high-pitched sing-song tone.

He turned around to see Bridget Drake standing there, a little wet from the rain, her curly brown hair streaking across her face. John could see her nipples protruding a little from her black shirt that clung tightly to her chest.

"Er, hi Bridget," he said uncomfortably. He had been frequently warned not to talk to her. Most kids in the town had been advised against it after an incident a few years ago where Bridget had been found in a neighbour's garden, gnawing on the remains of their dead dog's leg.

"It's so wet," she commented, licking her lips and moving towards him.

"Yeah. I got locked out."

"Me too," she replied. Bridget had always lived with her Aunt and it seemed unlikely that she would not have her own key at her age, but John decided not to think too hard about it.

"I sometimes like to come here. To think. You know?" he said, trying to be sociable and yet change the subject, at the same time.

"Me too," she replied, a strange smile forming on her face that disarmed him a little. He had been warned that she could be unpredictable.

"I think I have to get going soon though, I guess my parents'll be home," he said, standing up and hoping that Bridget didn't notice the bulge he was still harbouring in the front of his pants. The sight of her hardened nipples beneath the fabric had done nothing to get rid of it.

"Oh don't go. Stay a bit."

"Nah, I really should be…" he began, about to edge past her when she thrust her hand down towards his crotch and began to stroke.

"You like?"

He couldn't deny that the feeling was pleasant. She had almost unnaturally long fingers and, as she rubbed them up and down in his groin, he felt himself merely gasping for breath in response to her question. He looked at her. She was undeniably attractive, in spite of her spooky eyes, he thought. She moved her face to his and kissed him.

"Wait…" he begged, implicitly.

He momentarily thought of Sarah but her image dissolved as he felt Bridget's skilful hand unbuttoning his trousers and freeing his cock. It sprung out forcefully and she sent down a second hand to caress it, all the while her tongue flicking around wildly in his mouth. He moved his hands to cup her breasts and tried to return the kiss as best he could. He was inexperienced and still a little dazed from how fast everything had happened, so his tongue merely flopped about aimlessly in her warm mouth. She tasted faintly of almonds.

After what seemed like a blissful eternity to him, she moved her hands up to his chest and ripped open the buttons of his school shirt, flinging it to the wet, muddy ground below. At this point, she removed her own shirt and skirt gracefully, revealing nothing underneath except a lean, perfectly formed body, as John, almost in a trance, clumsily took his trousers off. She slowly knelt down, running her fingers down his chest as she moved, eventually lining up her mouth with his crotch. He let out a brief shriek of unexpected ecstasy as she wrapped her lips around the head of his cock and swiftly sucked the whole shaft into the welcoming heat of her mouth.

He felt that wicked tongue of hers moving frenziedly around, as his mind became completely blank, concentrating on nothing beyond the feeling of exquisite pleasure she was giving to him. He barely even noticed the sudden flood of hot liquid that filled her mouth, the stinging pleasure gradually becoming intense pain, then numbness… then…?

He looked down and saw that she had detached herself from his crotch. Dark, crimson liquid was spurting in fountains from the gaping hole she had left above his testicles. He screamed, momentarily paralysed with the shock as the realisation set in of what had happened. He looked at her. She was spitting out more of his blood and he saw the last few centimetres of his penis disappear into her throat as she swallowed hard. Her eyes were glowing a ghastly yellow in the darkness now and he saw, as she flicked her tongue out at him, that it was forked down the middle.

"Fuck! FUCK!" he shrieked and grasped at his school shirt, pushing it into his crotch, a vain attempt to mop up the bleeding.

She moved her hand down to between her legs and began rubbing furiously at herself, yelping and panting with pleasure as he scrambled around and stumbled towards the briars, desperate to escape, but barely able to run, through all the pain. As he turned round to look at her, he saw she was convulsing now in pleasure, as she rubbed herself faster than before. He glanced at her throat and noticed something so hideous that he felt his consciousness begin to ebb away in horrified reaction.

He saw the outline of his own cock, slowly becoming erect within her throat, as she made herself more aroused. A long, fleshy protrusion, threatening to burst out of her skin, a monstrous mutation. She laughed as it reached its full length and sprang upwards from her neck. He stumbled, screamed and fell over, face down into the briars, soon feeling her leap onto his back.

"Mmm... mmm..."

She whispered sounds of pleasure into his ear and he felt the hard shaft of his own cock rubbing against his shoulder from within the folds of her neck. Her hands moved swiftly, grabbing thorny branches from the briars and binding him into the brambles. He was blacking out now and beyond feeling the pain of the thorns tearing through the tender, young flesh of his wrists.

When he was firmly bound, he felt her again on his back and could feel that ghastly, unnatural appendage moving slowly down his spine, from his neck down to between his buttocks. He screamed as he felt it plunge mercilessly into him with one almighty thrust, an excruciating pain that could be felt even with the last veils of consciousness slowly falling away. It thrust in and out with inhuman speed, over and over again, ripping his anus to bloody tattered shreds, peeling open the fleshy ruins of his colon and soiling his buttocks with shit and gore. Life was draining rapidly from him, pouring out in scarlet rivers from between his legs. He felt her brown hair whipping his back with the motion of her head going up and down. It was the last thing John Piper would ever feel, as his body became limp and lifeless, dangling from the brambles like a torn-up rag doll.

The old woman approached the scene from within the darkness, an otherworldly glow surrounding her silver hair. Her yellow eyes glowed in the night as she spoke to Bridget. "The sixth virgin is thus defiled," she intoned.

Bridget detached herself from the broken remains of John Piper and turned to face the crone. The hard cock still shot outwards from her throat, like some ghastly, oversized Adam's apple. She lifted her head and, with a rattling gurgle, spat it out. It landed flaccid and quite dead into the mud, her throat returning to an ordinary, human shape once more.

"The cycle is nearly complete," the crone said. "Come, we must be rid of this filthy flesh."

Bridget laughed and raised her face to the sky, letting the rain wash her face clean of all the blood, skin and excrement that had spattered it. The crone approached her and kissed her on the lips, tasting the last remains of it.

"You are such a good girl."

PART TWO: SEX AND MAGIC

The Hidden Circles
A Ruse Uncovered

"Are you not the oasis where I dream, and the gourd from which I drink in long draughts the wine of memory?"
– Charles Baudelaire

VIII

Jeff knocked on the door of Peter's room at the Bull's Head Inn. His brother came to the door, looking the worse for wear. His blond hair was tousled and dirty. He had a visible cut across his lip and a fresh bruise forming around his left eye.

"Oh my God, what the Hell happened?" asked Jeff.

"I don't know. What happened to you? Where the fu-c-k-k-k were you last night anyway?" Peter rubbed his eye and winced.

"God, Peter, I'm sorry. I had to go. I found something out about Dad. I … I… Jesus. Who did this to you?"

Peter let Jeff into the small, pokey, brown room as he began to explain, in a loud tone of voice that was dripping thickly with sarcasm. "Well, I think-k I found out the same stuff you did about Dad. Just maybe the slightly harder way."

"What happened?"

"I went into the Old C-c-c-crown to meet you and you weren't there. So I said hi to Taverner and ordered a pint, when these two old blo-k-kes in the corner came over and started mouthing off. Lik-k-k-ke father, li-k-ke son, they were saying and all that shit."

"You know why?"

"Oh yeah, they told me all that too! The one guy said that Dad had k-k-k-killed some little girl. That he was fuc-k-k-king her and he were a dirty old c-c-c-cunt. Said the whole family were scum. Then the bastard hit me in the eye."

"Jesus…" Jeff closed his eyes.

"Yeah, I hit him back of c-c-course. But then his mate piled in. Hit me in the ribs and I went down for another one

45

in the face." He pointed to his swollen lip. "At that point, Taverner break-k-ks it up and tells me I should leave. So I went and got some chips from the chippie instead. Ate them in the room. Figured you weren't c-c-c-oming anyway." He waved his hand dismissively.

"I'm sorry. I got so mad that Jenny hadn't said anything about Dad. I needed to hear it from her."

"And?"

"And it's true. We sat down and talked about it. She said she wanted to tell me, to tell us, but she just didn't know how to."

"So he k-k-killed that girl?"

"No. Not that bit. Well, we don't know that either way I suppose. But it seems unlikely. Jenny did say it was weird though, that he was hanging around the girl a lot for a month or so before she died. She said she just tried to ignore it, pass it off as harmless. She never saw him act at all untoward with the girl, just said he was maybe 'having a second fatherhood', was the exact words she used."

"And the night she disappeared?"

"Jenny didn't even see him that night, nor the girl. He just said he was going out and went."

Peter took a deep breath and held his hand to his eye.

"Looks like it hurts," remarked Jeff.

"Yeah, it does. I'd forgotten what this town was like. To think-k I thought I was having a hard time in London, with not getting a job and all that. At least that's the best thing about the bloody place. You can just be anonymous. Most people in the city, just walk-k-king about, they don't know or care who you are or… what you've done."

"Yeah."*Or what you haven't done*, thought Jeff of himself, wondering if the population of London would so much as bat an eye at his singularly uneventful, dreary life, even if it were printed up in great detail and broadcast on the screens of Piccadilly Circus in nightly instalments.

"Up here, you c-c-c-can't walk anywhere without getting dirty looks. I'll be glad when we get shot of the place again."

"Fancy a fry-up? We can go to Meg's caf', if you want."

"Oh sure. I love a bit of spit and phlegm with my break-k-kfast."

"They won't spit in it. Those guys in the bar last night were overreacting. Probably just drunk. Blaming you for what they reckon Dad did."

"No they weren't. They were blaming me for what *I* did. Everyone in this town knows where I was for the last two C-C-Christmases. Lik-ke father, li-k-k-ke son."

"Don't say that."

"About Dad or about me?"

"About Dad, Peter." Jeff turned away from his brother to face the door. "You know full well what you are."

"Yeah, I do." He paused. "I think I'll sk-kip on that break-kfast."

"Ok. Well, I'll be at Meg's for a few hours if you want me."

There was uncomfortable silence. Peter opened the paisley curtains and stared out of the window at the street below. An old lady with a shopping bag was the only life out there. Jeff motioned towards the door.

"I'm sorry I just said that," he began, turning back to face his brother. "I wish... I wish... I wish I understood what had happened to us."

"Nothing happened to you, Jeff. Nothing ever has," Peter spat. "You just go through your neat and tidy city life without worrying about it. Nice job, nice flat. Nice fuck-k-king life."

Jeff was slightly stunned by his brother's sudden aggression. "What are you saying? Are you...? Oh my God. Did Dad ever...?"

"Oh for God's sake. Don't be stupid. Dad never touched me."

"Then what? What went so wrong?"

"Just life, Jeff," he said, staring his brother in the eye. "Just life."

There was another uncomfortable silence. Jeff wanted to scream at his brother. To tell him to stop being so self-pitying and pathetic. When their mother died, they were 17 and 18 years old. Jeff had dropped out of University and begun to work as an apprentice in the HBG warehouse in Balham. Peter had *chosen* to do nothing and now he was claiming he was hard done by. They had both started out in the same place. Still, Jeff bit his tongue and breathed deeply. He didn't say any of this to his brother because, if he was honest, he was afraid of this man; this capricious stranger that stood in front of him.

"Yeah, it's a bitch," was all he said, turning and slamming the door as he left.

IX

Mrs Hobson was up early that morning, as the whole house could tell from the strangulated screaming coming from her room. Mr Hobson had gone in, hauled her out of bed and sat her in her chair. He then wheeled her to the stair lift.

By 7am, Mrs Hobson had been sat in her favourite position, in front of the TV, watching the breakfast news, her head lolling to one side. Her bowl of porridge lay untouched beside her. Mr Hobson had tried feeding it to her but she wouldn't open her mouth. She was clearly in one of her obstinate moods today.

Sarah went back to sleep and got up again at 8am, when her alarm rang. She washed, ate a hurried breakfast of cornflakes and toast, then changed into her school uniform.

"Oh 'ello Sarah," her dad said, as she entered the living room. "Did you 'ear your mam this morning?"

"Yes," she replied, glancing at her mother, who sat motionless in the wheelchair by the TV. "So what's wrong with her this morning then?"

"She's having one of 'er funny turns I think. Would you mind giving 'er a bath later, love? When you get 'ome from school, like?"

"Fine," Sarah grumbled although it was actually anything but. It occasionally pained her to admit it, but she resented having to care for a mother who had never been capable of caring for her. Mrs Hobson had experienced a severe stroke when Sarah had been only three years old and this was the only state in which she ever remembered seeing her. Mr Hobson had insisted on caring for his wife at home and had arranged for the NHS to install the stair lift and special bathroom in the house. Since Sarah turned twelve, two years previously, he had been putting an increasing onus on her to help with the looking after of her mother. Sarah found the whole business disgusting. Her mother's pasty, pimply flesh reminded her of the chickens her dad brought home from his butcher shop. She hated touching it.

"I have to go now," she said and left without saying goodbye. It pained her to act this way to her father, whom she loved deep down, but some days he just took advantage and it made her nearly sick with anger.

On the way to the bus stop, she saw Jeff Davies walking from the Bull's Head Inn towards Meg's Café. He smiled weakly and she ignored him. She had read in the papers about his father being involved with Katie Brown's disappearance. Secretly, she found this fascinating. It was the closest Broadoak had come to having a decent news story in her lifetime, if not ever. The local paper, usually full of awards for farmers with oversized fruits, annoyingly swotty school project coverage, announcements of fortieth birthday parties and royal family visits to Gloucester, was suddenly worth reading.

She had met the dead man, Guy Davies, a few times and never thought of him as being anything beyond a fairly normal, boring old man. He occasionally came round to see her parents and stayed for tea. Sarah would usually disappear upstairs with a tray and leave Guy and her dad to talk by themselves. She paid as little attention as possible to what went on in the world of Broadoak's grown-ups. She was terrified of one day becoming one of them. She already knew that as soon as she was old enough she would leave Broadoak and move to a real town or, better yet, a proper city.

For once, John Piper did not appear at the bus stop this morning to interrupt her thoughts and dreams. This was a relief. His pathetic teenage obsession with her was starting to really grate on her nerves. She had no time for any of the boys at school, they were all useless and childish. She pulled a copy of William Burroughs's *'Naked Lunch'* from her bag and began to read, waiting for the bus to show up.

Back at the house, her father received a letter in the post; a plain black envelope. He opened it and found a dried tulip petal and an all too familiar symbol inside. The symbol depicted two silver serpents, entwined. He stared at it for a few seconds and then showed it to his wife, who made a vile, gargling noise in response. They both began to weep.

"It's happening," he said, between sobs. "It's really happening."

X

On the way to the café, Jeff walked past Flowers By Ethyl, the local florist. Ethyl herself was outside, unlocking the door and adjusting the 'OPEN' sign. Jeff smiled to himself. It still amazed him how much Ethyl looked like the archetypal 'little old lady'. She was barely five-foot tall and as skinny as a rake. She wore her woolly grey hair up in a tight bun above her head and balanced bifocal spectacles on her crooked, crinkled nose. She wore a thick blue anorak to shelter her from the rain, still spitting after last night's downpour, and a long black skirt. Jeff could never remember her looking any different.

He had never known his real grandmother and Ethyl, being a close friend of the family, had treated him, Peter and Jenny like the grandchildren she had never had, whenever they saw her. He had been meaning to drop by her shop to say hello later anyway but decided now was as good a time as any.

"Jeffrey!" she exclaimed, hobbling across to him. She craned her neck and kissed his cheek.

"Hiya, how's things?" he asked, unable to suppress the grin that was forming across his face upon seeing her.

"Oh, it could be better, dear. I'm still very shaken by what happened to Guy."

"Yeah. I'm sorry I haven't come to see you before. I just, well, the last twenty four hours have been a bit…"

"I understand. Do come in, love, have a cup of tea."

Jeff followed her into the shop and was hit by the strong, dizzying scent of flowers. His nose began to tickle slightly and he surreptitiously rubbed it whilst Ethyl wandered into the back room.

"White, two sugars still, yes?"

"Yes, ta."

She soon came out, clutching two cups with primitive floral designs on them, nearly overflowing with hot brown tea.

"So, I suppose you know all the rumours by now, dear. About Guy."

"Yeah, I heard last night. Taverner told me."

"Oh my," Ethyl looked quite shocked. "I'd at least have thought Jenny might've warned you about it before you got here."

"No. I found out the hard way. Well, actually, no. *Peter* found out the hard way. A couple of local blokes decked him in the pub last night."

Ethyl gasped. "Oh my. I am sorry. Poor Peter."

"Yeah. Whichever way you slice it, that was bang out of order. I... I still can't quite work it all out though. Did you ever see Dad with this Katie girl?"

"Of course I did and it was perfectly harmless, let me tell you that, dear. It's all just symptomatic of this ridiculous day and age. A man can't even show the slightest bit of fatherly kindness to a little girl without being accused of all sorts of disgusting filth."

"So it's nonsense then?"

"Yes it's nonsense, Jeffrey. Didn't you know your father at all?"

There was a pause, as Jeff thought about this question for longer than he probably should have done.

"I guess not."

Ethyl's face fell. "Oh, Jeffrey."

"I'm sorry. I just guess I didn't really. I only saw him once a year. Maybe twice if he was in London for something."

"Well, I knew your father and I knew him well. He was a good man. He shouldn't have had to die like that."

"But what actually happened that night? He just fell in the river?"

"I don't know. The police are investigating it and I'd

rather just leave it to them. Whatever happened was a terrible accident and a great loss to everyone who knew him."

"What about the girl? Katie? Do you think she's still alive?"

Ethyl's eyes crinkled and she looked with genuine sadness at Jeff. "I don't even want to think what might have happened to that poor lamb. She was only eight years old. I can only expect that she was washed away with the current of the river."

"But the police haven't found her yet."

"The Severn isn't exactly small, Jeffrey."

"I know, I know. It's just... I don't know. Something doesn't fit."

Ethyl took Jeff's hand in hers. "Sometimes things don't fit. When you reach my age, a lot of people you know and love are dead and it doesn't make sense why some stay and others leave earlier than they should do. Our Lord moves in mysterious ways."

Jeff smiled, humouring her. He had little to no time for religion.

"Do not dwell on why things happen. Just hold on to what good memories you do have of your father. Think about them tomorrow at the funeral. It will be as if he is there himself, in spirit. But he is with the Lord now."

Jeff dislodged his hand, gently, from Ethyl's and drained the remainder of his cup of tea. "I know. Thanks."

"How is Peter?"

"Heh. Bruised, but otherwise ok. He seems a bit more stable than he has been."

"I do suppose he had a lot of time to think during his time away."

"Yeah. Prison has definitely mellowed him."

"Well, do tell him he's welcome to stop by for a cup of tea any time he likes. I imagine he could do with seeing a friendly face."

"Yeah, thanks. I'll tell him if I see him."

"Not everyone in Broadoak wants to force him to atone, my dear. Our Lord forgives those who wander from the flock and we should do so too."

"I know," Jeff said quietly, stealing a look at his watch. "Anyway, I better get going, I've got a ton of stuff to get on with."

"I can well imagine. Do try not to listen to what they say about your father. Be strong, Jeffrey."

"Heh, I'll try. Cheers for the tea. I'll see you tomorrow at the funeral?"

"Of course you will."

"Thanks, Ethyl. I appreciate your being there for us."

XI

Peter Davies stayed in bed for the duration of the morning. His head was aching and his body was sore all over. He felt slightly nauseated by midday for having not eaten yet but he didn't feel like getting up again. He wanted to block out the sunlight; block out the whole cursed town. He had no desire to go out there and walk along the street, to be stared at, looked down upon, and damned by the lot of them. He began wondering why he had even come here in the first place. He had barely known his father in life and felt curiously little about his death. It had been a strange sense of familial duty and bitter obligation that had dragged him here. That coupled with the fact that he had been craving a change of scenery, no matter what the circumstances.

He had been driving himself crazy, stuck in his Stockwell bedsit, watching the hours pass away whilst desperately trying to rid himself of the urges that would land him another two year stretch in the nick. The evening work at the chip shop was pure drudgery but, by comparison to fighting the demons in his own mind, it came as sweet relief. The twice weekly therapy sessions were helping, but all too slowly, and he still felt judged when he sat there trying to rationalise the irrational; the primal, animalistic instincts inside him. The ones that worsened each time he caught sight of a pretty young girl.

He was hoping that by getting out of London for a few days, it might refresh him and help him relax but already he was longing to be back in the anonymous bustling crowds of the capital where he could become virtually invisible. Nothing was worse to him than the feeling of being looked on as scum. He had spent two gruelling years enduring just that. Even men who were far more evil, cruel and violent saw him as the lowest rung on the ladder. They didn't know the full story. They didn't even bother to ask first. They just knew what the judge had said and anything at all to do with children seemed to raise the hackles on even the hardest of hard knocks. A tattooed man who had been convicted of the robbery and murder of a couple of pensioners had kicked Peter to within an inch of his life in his first week of prison, all the while yelling and attesting his own moral superiority. It was a jumbled-up world in there and now he was feeling it all over again in Broadoak with the men in the pub. Peter wondered if English small town life wasn't a prison in itself. He silently gave thanks to his mother for taking him and Jeff out of it while they were still too young to notice.

For all the good it did me.

He looked at his watch and saw that it was already 3pm. He had wanted to go and see Jenny, but hadn't quite mustered up the courage. Something told him he should attempt to make peace with his estranged sister prior to the funeral, but it was difficult to know where to begin. They had not spoken a word since three Christmases ago; the last one before Peter's conviction. She had made no effort to contact him since then and the message had been clear; she wanted nothing more to do with him ever again.

Peter wished he could run away and hide from all of this. He was happiest when no one was around him at all and there was no chance of conflict. But he knew he had spent his whole life running and it had got him nowhere. Groaning and wincing with pain as he stood up, Peter knew it was time to bite the bullet. Within fifteen minutes he had washed, dressed, and was at the top of Nailsworth Road, ready to face his sister.

He knocked at the door and she answered it promptly. She was dressed in an old lumberjack shirt and jeans, clutching and flicking an unlit cigarette in her hand like a rosary.

"Jennifer," he began. His mouth felt suddenly dry and it was a struggle to open it.

"What do you want? Why are you here? Do you think I actually want to see you?" she spoke softly but with a definitive sneer of contempt.

"I just thought it might be a good idea to c-c-c-clear the air before Dad's funeral," he said, unable to quite meet her eyes as they stared viciously at him.

"Peter, I'm sorry you even came to Broadoak this weekend, let alone to my house. Do you even know what they're saying about Dad?"

"Yes, I've... heard."

"Where do you think that idea comes from?"

"Well, probably the fact that he was spending so much time around that little girl, from what I hear..."

"Oh don't be stupid. There was nothing in it. No one would've even thought that if it wasn't for you and what you did!"

"Jenny, that's not fair."

"You know, I couldn't even understand, I couldn't even... even... think about what you did. I can't reconcile it to anything that's ever happened in our family. Yet now I'm sat here having doubts about my own fucking father because of it. What have you done to us?"

"Jenny, whatever Dad's done, if it was anything at all, it's nothing to do with me or you or anyone. It's his own business."

"Peter. You're sick. You're a sick, horrible man. How the Hell can you stand there and try to moralise to me?"

"Jenny…"

"Peter, you're a child molester. A bloody monster."

Peter felt a chill in his blood and began to shake a little. He didn't quite know what to say, how to explain himself. He wished he could find the eloquence to explain himself to his sister. "Jenny, I never touched her. I never touched any

58

of them. Anyone. Ever. I…"

"Peter, I don't want to hear it. I don't even want you to try and justify anything you've done. I'm not even interested." She began to close the front door.

"Jenny, I c-c-c-can't explain why. I just want you to know, I never touched…"

"She was twelve years old, Peter! Twelve years old! A child!"

"I… I…"

"You! You, you, you! That's all it's ever about! She was twelve years old. Think about her for a change. How do you think the image of your filthy cock poking out of the bushes is going to affect her? Do you think about her? The way her life might be in five, ten years time?"

"Not a day goes by when I don't feel sick-k about what I did… but Jenny…"

"Peter, just go. I have things to do. I'm not interested in hearing your feeble apologies. Just go drown in that pathetic guilt of yours."

She slammed the door. He punched it lightly and yelled incoherently. He stood there, hoping Jenny would return but when she didn't, he soon sidled away, heading down Nailsworth Road miserably and berating himself for having handled the entire confrontation so poorly. The rain had stopped but there was a biting wind beginning to nip at his earlobes. Typical English weather. He had no desire to walk back through town and decided to head down to the riverbank.

The ground was muddy and he was not expecting to see any people on his way. Occasionally he knew people would walk their dogs along the bank's paths but in this weather he found it was unlikely. It took him by surprise when he saw the girl sat on the bank in her school uniform, headphones in her ears, smoking what appeared to be a hand-rolled cigarette. He decided to walk past and not even look at her, but as he approached, she turned round, slightly startled, flicked her headphones out of her ears and nodded up at him.

"Hey," she said.

"Hi." He recognised her now as Sarah Hobson, but hadn't seen her for a good many years. She had changed her physical appearance somewhat since then and blossomed into an attractive young girl, something he tried hard not to think about as he smiled weakly in greeting.

"Nice day for a walk?" she chirped.

"I guess."

There was a brief silence and Peter, still angry and not in the mood for small talk nor introductions, decided to cut her down. "Haven't you been told not to talk-k to me?"

"No."

"Oh."

"I mean," she continued, smiling a little cruelly, "I don't really need to be told. Everyone knows who you are. It kind of goes without saying."

"Oh." Peter was a little stunned by the girl's attitude. He'd been expecting her to react to his presence with fear or disgust, but instead she seemed almost amused by him.

"Not much of a talker, I take it?"

"I don't know. Most people don't talk-k to me, so I don't get much chance to flex-x my conversational muscle."

"Shame. You and your dad are about the most interesting story to ever come out of Broadoak."

"An interesting story? I'm glad you think so." Peter didn't know whether to be offended or delighted by the girl's audacity, but found himself suppressing a grin nonetheless. He decided to see how far she would take the conversation, thus sat down beside her on the riverbank, stretching dramatically and craning his head to watch the sun set behind a curtain of murky clouds and the bare, shaking branches of the trees.

"So what's London like?" Sarah asked, apropos of nothing.

"London? Um. It's nothing like Broadoak."

Sarah flopped back onto the grass dramatically and exhaled a sigh of relief. "Thank fuck. This place is such shite. I can't wait to leave."

"You want to go to London?"

"Maybe London, maybe Birmingham, maybe just Gloucester or Cardiff, I don't know. Anywhere that's not shite I suppose."

"London c-c-can be pretty shite."

"Not like this though, surely?"

"No. Not like this." Peter smiled. "At least in London no one knows who you are. You c-c-can just slip into the street like part of this big flow of people and no one sees you."

"Sounds like Heaven," murmured Sarah. "Do you smoke?" she asked, pulling a small polythene bag of marijuana from her pocket.

"I think it's probably in violation of my parole."

Sarah laughed hysterically. "My God, could you *be* any less dangerous?"

Peter smiled against his will. On one hand, he felt his pride faintly wounded but on the other, this was the first time someone had treated him like a normal, everyday person instead of an inhuman monster for some years now.

"It's probably in violation of my parole," she jeered in a sing-song voice that mocked his. "Come on, it's just a joint and for God's sake, who's going to see you here? I want you to tell me all about London."

"Oh, alright then. What do you want to know?"

Sarah swiftly began rolling a joint, a well-practiced motion that she performed more or less subconsciously. "I dunno. Like, where's your favourite place in London?"

Peter chuckled. "God, I don't know. Where's your favourite place in Broadoak?"

"Probably here," replied Sarah, matter-of-factly. "It's the only place I can come to think. Get away, y'know?"

"I know. You'd miss somewhere lik-ke this in London. It's not the greenest place, overall."

"I'd live. So? What's your favourite place?"

"Hmmm. I really lik-ke the West End. Soho, Charing C-c-c-cross Road, all that."

"I've never been. What are they like?"

"Pretty squalid to tell the truth. There are always loads of people and there's all these little dumpy shops down Tottenham C-court Road that sell cheap electric-ccal goods. The shop fronts are all dirty and on a weekend you c-c-an barely move for all the c-c-crowds but I guess I just find it so fascinating. You look up and the buildings are so tall. There are so many people in there. I find myself wondering what they're doing. It's li-k-ke all of London happens in secret. Behind the doors of these big gothic monstrosities. I love it. The mystery of it all."

"Wow, sounds well cool," Sarah said, lighting up the joint and taking the first, long drag. "I don't know as anything secret happens in Broadoak. If it did it'd be shite."

"I dunno. I sometimes feel a bit uneasy here."

"Uneasy?"

"Yeah, I guess I'm just used to living in a big city. It feels like I'm being watched all the time here, by everyone. It mak-k-kes me feel on edge."

"What? You think someone's going to leap out of the shadows? Maybe Mrs Deering from the sweet shop might spring from behind the bon bon jars and attack you with liquorice snakes!" Sarah made a hissing sound and raised her hands up. "Actually," she said, noticing his black eye. "Is that what happened to you?"

"This? Nah, this was a c-couple of twats in the Old C-c-crown last night."

"Gutted. Here, this ought to ease the pain." Sarah handed him the joint and he looked down at her hand as he took it, noticing her silver ring. He recoiled slightly.

"Woah, where did you get that?" he asked, suddenly ignoring the joint.

"I found it. Why?"

"*Where* did you find it?"

"Down here, by the river actually. A couple of days ago. Why?"

"My dad, he had one just lik-ke it."

Sarah turned away and, seeing Peter had lost interest in the joint, took another long drag. "I see," she said.

"What's wrong?"

"Nothing. I just got some smoke in my eye."

"You really found this by the river?"

"Yes."

"I think it might be my dad's ring. Do you mind if I have a look?"

Sarah reluctantly slipped the ring off her finger and handed it to Peter, who began to examine it in detail. The silver serpents looked remarkably like the ones on his father's ring and, when he looked on the inside of the band, he noticed the initials GD engraved there. "Look!" he shouted. "It's got my dad's initials on it!"

Sarah looked nervous all of a sudden. "I didn't know whose it was."

"It's ok-k. I'm not blaming you for tak-k-king it. You found a ring on the floor, it's c-c-cool. Finders, k-keepers and all that."

"No, it's not that."

"Then what?"

"You'll think I'm fucked up if I tell you."

"Jesus, look who you're talk-k-king to. I *am* the town fuck-k-up. I'm really in no position to judge." He smiled.

"It was… on someone's hand."

"Eh? You mean, on my dad's hand? On the body, before they found it?"

"No. I didn't know whose it was, like I say. The hand was… by itself."

Peter's face dropped. "Where… where did you find this… hand?"

Sarah stood up and pointed to a part of the riverbank that spread out before a small alcove of bushes. "Over there."

Peter walked over to the alcove and began to scan the bushes. It was too dark to see anything. "Give me your lighter," he demanded and Sarah tossed it over to him without question. Her features had become suddenly pale and nervous, as though she suddenly realised what she had done. The hand was no longer just anonymous meat. Plus, if it had indeed belonged to Guy Davies, this was a whole new story. She felt already as though she were in a little deeper than she'd like to be, as she watched Peter scrambling in the bushes with his lighter.

"I can't find anything," he said.

"With all the rain last night, I guess the river overflowed a bit. The bank's still all wet. It probably got washed away."

"Shit."

"I'm sorry." She wasn't entirely sure what for, but it felt like the right thing to say.

"You aren't lying are you? You really found this ring on a… severed hand?"

"Seriously."

"How the Hell would he lose his hand, falling into a river?"

"I don't know. I…"

"I have to go." He gave her the lighter and the ring back.

"Hey. Don't you want this? If it was your dad's…"

"No. You k-k-keep it."

Peter began to walk away.

"Hey, where are you going?" she yelled after him.

"I have to see my brother."

XII

Jeff was alone in the house and it felt strange. Jenny had disappeared some hours earlier, as soon as Jeff had returned from town. She had a date apparently, which Jeff thought peculiar, as she had never mentioned a boyfriend before this point. That said, considering how little they actually talked to one another about their lives, it was probably no surprise that the subject had not been broached. The smell of the old house was oppressive and was making Jeff melancholy.

He put the kettle on and went to make a cup of tea, smiling as he took out the first mug to hand, one he had given his father some twenty years ago. The design was faded and there was a large chip in the rim, but you could still read the "World's Greatest Dad" print on the side. Jeff dwelt on how strange it was, the things you buy as children, the sentiments you long to express whether they're true or not. A child's grasp of affection towards their parents is a curious, largely unrequited one. Jeff couldn't remember when he had reached the age when suddenly he realised his dad was a cold recluse whom he barely saw and who meant nothing to him. But now, holding the tea mug in his hand, amazed and bemused that his father had kept it all these years, Jeff began wondering if he even knew the man at all and if maybe he had been unfair, judging him as one would almost judge a stranger.

Sipping the tea, he began wandering around the living room, trying to conjure the ghosts of Christmases past, but failing. They had always been amiable enough, with Jenny cooking a meal and his dad buying cheap crackers. The whole family, or what was left of it, would sit beneath the glow of the fairy lights on the little artificial tree. That was about as close as they were ever likely to get; affable enough, yet they wouldn't ever really talk about anything real. They'd perhaps discuss current events, they'd tell the jokes from the crackers, they'd gossip momentarily about what was happening in Broadoak and yet Jeff didn't even know, prior to tonight, whether or not Jenny had a boyfriend.

He ran his hand along the small, imitation mahogany desk in the corner of the room and found he was unable to resist a peek inside. The key was left in the drawer and he felt so lost and so anxious to gain some vague insight into the internal mechanisms of what passed for his family, that any guilt or apprehension dissolved as quickly as the sugar in his tea had done. Sliding open the creaky old drawer, he was confronted by unpaid electricity bills, a pamphlet from the local Conservative Party and a plain black envelope with a letter inside.

He checked the back of the envelope and found it had already been opened. Lifting up the contents, he was disappointed to find a dried tulip petal and a single sheet of paper with a hand painted symbol on it that meant absolutely nothing to him. It looked a little like a figure eight with scales. Perhaps it was Japanese, he thought, putting it back with the feeling that he was more puzzled now than when he began. He resigned himself to the fact that his sister and his father would probably always be a mystery to him and, with that, sat down on the couch feeling thoroughly dejected.

The telephone rang.

"Hello?" he said, picking up the receiver with a distinct tone of doubt in his voice.

The voice on the line was throaty, speaking rapidly in a language Jeff didn't recognise. He only caught the word "Jennifer" at which he responded, "It's Jeff, her brother. Can I help?"

The caller hung up.

He was surprised when, minutes later, he heard the

doorbell ring. He put his mug of tea down and went to answer it. Peter stood at the door, a shock of his blond hair cascading down his face, which was whiter than usual. His eyes were wide-awake.

"Jeff. I think there's something seriously weird about Dad's death."

"Huh? Weird how?"

"Do you know Sarah Hobson?"

"Err, yeah. I saw her yesterday actually."

"I saw her today. She was wearing Dad's ring. On her finger."

"Are you sure?"

"I took it off and had a good look. It even had his initials c-c-carved on the inside. It was definitely his. Don't you remember? The one with the silver snakes that he always used to wear?"

"Oh shit, that old thing, yeah. I do vaguely remember that. I always figured he got it in one of those cheap crackers he used to buy for Christmas." Jeff giggled at his own joke but Peter's face remained sombre.

"I asked her where she got it."

"And?"

"She said she found it by the river."

"Well, that would make sense, given he drowned in it."

"She said she took it off a severed hand she found there."

Jeff cocked an eyebrow. "A severed hand?"

"Yes."

"And you believe this girl?"

"Yes. I know it sounds stupid, but seriously. She had Dad's ring."

"But the hand thing... that's stretching it. I mean, she is a bit freaky, do you not think she might just have a morbid, overactive imagination?"

"I don't know. Maybe it's me that has one too, but there's

something weird about it don't you think?"

"Fine, you want to tell the police?"

"Oh, fuck-k-k off."

Jeff laughed. They both had a history of dislike for the local police sergeant, Owen MacRae. He was typical of the small-town xenophobe mentality and tried to create hassle almost every year for the brothers when they visited. He would give Jeff parking tickets on the car or breathalyse him when he saw him driving. He had taken an even deeper dislike to Peter and given him several invasive pat-down searches even before his conviction. He would always make jokes about London, refer to them as The London Brothers and sing "London Calling" loudly to himself when he walked past them on the street. Both brothers doubted they would have much sympathy from the local police force with a fairly vague story like this to go on and that bastard MacRae presiding over it all.

"But think about it, Jeff," said Peter, his voice almost a whisper now. "What if she's telling the truth? How the Hell did Dad lose his hand? He drowned!"

There was a clicking sound and a scrape in the front door. "Shit!" hissed Peter. "That's Jenny, she'll k-kill me if she sees me here."

"Quick, get out the back door. It's unlocked!"

"What about...?"

"Shut up and go. I'll meet you down the bottom of the road in five minutes, ok?"

Peter made a run for the kitchen and managed to escape into the cover of darkness before Jenny had chance to see him. She came through the front door to see Jeff stood nonchalantly in the living room, mug of tea in hand, admiring a painting of a collie dog that hung above the television. He nearly dropped his tea when he noticed with whom she was entering the house. It was Sergeant Owen MacRae.

"Owen," he said by way of greeting, attempting to appear casual.

"Jeffrey. Ha ha!" Owen let out a mad shriek of laughter. "I heard you were up from the Big Smoke. You and the other London Brother. What's his name? Pedo?"

"Peter."

"Hey. Same difference." Jeff winced at this particular newspeak expression at the best of times, but it was made so much worse now by the fact that Owen MacRae was voicing it.

"So this is your date, Jen?"

"Yes, I've been seeing Owen for awhile," replied Jenny, lighting up a cigarette. "I would've told you but, well…"

"Yeah."

There was an awkward silence. Owen began to whistle "London Calling" by The Clash, nodding his oafish, oversized head. He was an old punk who'd grown up straight, yet a violent teenage rage still shone in his beady eyes. He still spiked his hair with gel but kept it at a respectable level, partly because of his job and partly because it was thinning so badly. He had gained weight since Jeff had last saw him and looked a little malformed now, as though his body was waterlogged. Everything about him set Jeff's nerves on edge. His teeth were jagged and horrible.

"You know," began Jeff, stretching his arms, "I think I'm going to head down the Crown for a pint or two. I'll be back later, ok?"

"Hey, do what you gotta," replied Owen, shrugging, even though he knew Jeff had not been addressing him.

"See you later, Jen."

Jeff strapped on his Barbour jacket and walked outside where it had begun to rain again. He found Peter stood at the end of the road, dripping wet already.

"Pint?" Jeff asked, smilingly.

"Pint and a fight in the C-c-crown again? No ta."

"Hmm, what do you suggest then? I said I was going down the pub."

"Grab some tins at the offy and c-c-come back to my room? We could use a bit of privacy. The walls have ears in the C-c-crown, I swear."

"Yeah, alright, why not?"

XIII

Sarah Hobson returned home just before the rain had begun. She had rerun the conversation with Peter Davies through her head several times on the way there. She was still amused by how the infamous Peter Davies, who had demonised in Broadoak for as long as she could remember, had been so innocuous in real life. Almost charming, even. His blue-grey eyes had been so piercing and the arc of his hair had flopped so gracefully across his forehead...

Stop it, Sarah.

She looked down at her fingers as she fumbled in her bag for a key to the house. How she wished she had never found the damn ring. If it wasn't for that, she could've continued the conversation longer with Peter Davies. How interesting it was to actually talk to someone who wasn't from Broadoak. Someone with something to say that wasn't mindless small town gossip. Someone who thinks further ahead than the next pint or the next football game or the next shopping trip to Gloucester on the train.

But she had obviously freaked him out. Of course she had. Stealing a ring from the severed hand of his father! God, it was ridiculous. She wondered how desensitised she must've become to normal human feelings for her to have taken it in the first place, cursing her father and his bloody butcher shop.

Slipping the key into the door, she entered the front room to find it empty, which was unusual. Normally on a Tuesday night, her father would be glued to "Panorama" on the TV. She heard voices coming from the kitchen and walked towards them, lured further by the smell of cooking. The voices suddenly stopped, as if aware that she was coming, and her father's head poked around the door. He was sweating even more than usual and his tubby face was flushed deep red.

"Oh, 'ello Sarah," he said. "I were just cooking up a bit of tea."

"Who's in there with you?"

"Oh, I invited a couple of your mum's friends over to join us tonight. Now, you go upstairs and this'll be all done with in about half hour, ok?"

"Ok." Sarah hesitated. It was very strange for her dad to send her upstairs. Usually he begged for her to stay with him and watch TV. It was also not standard practice in the Hobson household to entertain guests in the kitchen. "Is everything ok, Dad?"

"Of course, love." He smiled lopsidedly and she decided to leave him be. He did sometimes get into strange moods and had done so for as long as she could remember. Probably the burden of taking care of her mother took its toll on him once in awhile. She walked upstairs and began her nightly ritual of throwing her bag on her bed, changing clothes and rolling a joint.

She had just sparked up and was beginning to smoke when she heard raised voices coming from downstairs. Sneaking out onto the landing, Sarah listened hard, struggling to make out more than the odd word or two out of entire sentences.

"What happened before… don't even… how…"

It was a woman's voice, one that sounded faintly familiar.

"I can't, you know I can't…"

Her father's voice, broken and abnormally high-pitched.

"Broken… you know… family…"

The woman's voice again. Suddenly, Sarah heard the kitchen door fly open and slam. The woman's voiced called out "prepare to pay for it!", followed by footsteps stamping across the living room. It sounded like more than one person was storming out but Sarah could not tell for sure.

Her heart was beating fast now. The woman's voice had sounded incredibly severe. As soon as she heard the front door slam, she ran down to the kitchen to see her father.

He was sat at the table, head in hands, visibly weeping. There was a pot of vegetables on the stove. Boiling water from the pot was bubbling over onto the hob. Mrs Hobson sat in the wheelchair next to her husband, her face contorted into a horrific grimace. Mr Hobson was running his fingers nervously along the rim of a plain black envelope.

"Dad, what's wrong? Who was that?"

"Nothing, just a supplier," her dad replied, trying to regain composure, a little in vain.

"A supplier?"

"Yeah, an argument about payment. It's nothing. It'll pass. We're just going through a rough patch, with the bosted freezer and whatnot. There's not much money spare and I can't get a repairman in for love or money. Bloody health and safety'd close me down if they saw what were in there!"

"Dad..." Sarah actually felt genuine sympathy for the first time in awhile for her father. She went to put an arm around his sweaty, panting form. He swatted it away gently.

"No, Sarah, love," he said. "I've failed. I've really failed this time."

"You've not failed, Dad. Honest!" She tried to smile, but was feeling disorientated by the state of her father and the emotional roller coaster of the evening so far. He began to weep again.

"Look, don't worry," she said. "I'll fix dinner."

Walking towards the oven and turning down the hobs, she proceeded to do exactly that. It was the last meal she would ever make for her parents.

XIV

Jeff and Peter had picked up a six-pack of Carling Black Label from the local off license and were making their way up to the Bull's Head Inn. The rain had stopped almost as soon as it had begun, although the air remained chilly, damp, and thoroughly unwelcoming.

"I thought it'd be best to just sit in the room. They're having some k-k-kind of disco downstairs," said Peter. "Besides, I want to talk about Dad and I just don't trust that there's no one listening out here."

"Who the Hell would be stood out here in this weather, eavesdropping?"

"I don't know. I just k-keep getting this horrible feeling I'm being watched."

"Small town syndrome. I've been getting it myself but I figured it's fairly natural given we're so used to London."

They rounded the corner and saw the Bull's Head Inn, a modestly sized old Tudor building that looked rickety and unkempt. The lights in the downstairs bar were shining brightly through the gaps in the thick, paisley curtains. There was a black board propped up against the door that read 'FRIDAY NIGHT – MUSIC NIGHT – £1 a pint – Adnams Bitter' in big red chalk letters. There was a folksy bassline floating through the closed door.

Jeff went first and opened the door. The bar was busy. Around forty people were crammed into the small, dirty room, shuffling about on the brown and threadbare carpet. An elderly couple that Jeff didn't recognise were dancing slowly in the middle of the room as "Matchstalk Men and Matchstalk Cats and Dogs" blared hazily out of the speakers. Peter limped in behind Jeff and winced at the volume of chatter and music, pointing upwards and indicating with his head to the large oak door near the bar.

The two brothers smiled and nodded at various familiar faces as they snaked through the crowd and moved towards the door leading to the guest quarters. The rooms were located at the top of a precarious staircase that smelt of polish, ash and disinfectant. There were five bedrooms in the Bull's Head but rarely were more than one or two at a time ever occupied. Peter's room was number three and, as he slipped the key into the stiff and awkward lock mechanism, he heard Jeff pop open his first can of lager.

"God, I feel like I need this."

"Yeah, me too. Pass us one?"

Jeff handed a beer to his brother as they entered the room and sat down, Peter on the bed, Jeff on a wicker chair in the corner.

"I can't believe Jenny's seeing that twat MacCrae," barked Jeff as he took a large swill from his can.

"Yeah, that's a pisser. Wonder how long that's been going on?"

"Hm, she said it had been awhile."

"I wonder what she sees in him?"

"I dunno, but after all the shit he's put us two through you'd've thought she'd show some family loyalty."

"Nah, be fair. We live down there, she's up here. It's a completely different world. We're just those two strangers who bring her a new scarf or a tea mug at Christmas every year." Jeff mused, morosely.

"I don't think I really thought too much about Broadoak, y'know? About how different it is, living up here? I was tal-k-k-king to that Sarah Hobson today and she sounded so desperate to get out, to see something different. I suppose I tak-ke it for granted, bec-c-cause we moved to London so young. Never really understood what this place can do to a person."

"D'you reckon Jenny's gone a bit weird?"

"Jenny's always been a bit weird."

"Yeah, but the last few days. She seems so much more highly strung, even compared to usual."

"Look at her though. Her dad, who she lived with, is dead and she's going out with Owen bastard Mac-c-cRae. I'd be highly strung, in her position!"

Jeff laughed. "Yeah, I see what you mean."

"I don't think we should tell her about that thing with Dad's hand."

"Yeah. I'm still not entirely sure *what* I'd tell her."

Peter popped open his second can of lager, crushing the other in his hand and discarding it in the wicker bin by the side of the bed. "Why don't we find out for ourselves?"

"What?"

"Why don't we have a look-k-k at the old man? Check-k-k both hands are present and c-correct." He grinned, sardonically.

"We can't, the funeral's closed casket and then they're burying him. I don't think we're going to get much of a chance."

"Yeah, but what about tonight?" Peter had a glint his eye that Jeff had never seen before.

"I don't follow."

"He's laid out in the funeral parlour up the road. We c-c-could be in and out in half an hour. It's not even ten yet. It's Friday night. Half the town's downstairs, the other half's in the C-Crown or in bed. No one will even notice."

"You're saying we break into the funeral parlour?" Jeff took a long swig from his own lager, hoping it would help make what Peter was saying seem more rational.

"We're not going to tak-ke anything or move anything, I just want to see for myself. I mean, hey, it'd be nice to say goodbye to him face to face too, don't you think-k-k? I haven't seen him for three years, remember?"

"Oh, don't start using emotional blackmail to get me to agree to this. You're mad."

"Jeff, just think for a second. Let's say his hand *is* missing. There's definitely something someone somewhere isn't telling us if that's the c-c-case. But right now, we've got no proof of anything and if we let them bury him tomorrow, that's it. If there is something suspect going on, we've missed our chance." Peter was washing down beer hard and fast, drumming up Dutch courage as he popped open a third can.

"All you've got to go on is something a bloody schoolgirl told you. You're going to break into a funeral home for this?"

"I don't how else to emphasise this but we are *not* going to get c-c-c-caught."

"Famous last words, mate. Famous last words."

"You in? Or am I going by myself?"

"Friday nights in Broadoak are so slow, we have to hang out with the dead." Jeff popped another can of beer.

"Yes?"

"Go on then. I think I'd rather spend my time with rotting corpses than go home and see Owen MacRae again."

XV

Mrs Hobson awoke in her wheelchair. She did not remember how she got into it. Her surroundings were too dark for her to ascertain exactly where she was. Someone was pushing her across a carpet. Disorientated and scared, she whimpered and tried to recall events leading up to the present situation. Her last memory was of her husband scooping her out of the chair and laying her down in bed, kissing her goodnight and saying, "I'm sorry, love". She knew what for. She knew why. She knew something terrible would have to happen. She wished she had been able to speak, to offer her opinion on the situation. She would have done it differently than that weak-willed, bleeding heart husband of hers. She would've kept the pact. She already knew all too well what betrayal led to and eleven years imprisonment in this gaol of useless flesh and bone had hardened her. She found it tough to imagine how they could debase her or degrade her any further but confident they would find a way, she would've happily surrendered her ungrateful bitch daughter to them without hesitation.

The pushing stopped and a door was opened in front of her. With the light streaming in from the street, Mrs Hobson could now make out more clearly what was happening. She realised the door was to her own house and that she had been wheeled across the living room towards it. She could not see the person who was pushing her but she felt a jerky motion as she was forced out into the rainy street. She began to wail a little, helplessly, wishing that someone could hear her.

"Quiet, or I'll cut you," a spiteful, familiar voice whispered, almost gleefully. It was Bridget Drake, the half-wit girl, Mrs Hobson realised with terror.

Mrs Hobson struggled as the chair was pushed further down the street, and around the corner onto Monmouth

Street. She tried desperately to move her limbs, to escape, but nothing happened. The top of her head shook violently and her eyes darted around her, straining to find means of escape, hoping that someone would be walking by. She had no idea of the time but the icy cold temperature of the night sky indicated that it was late at night. Bitter raindrops stung the skin of her forehead as they pelted down. She closed her eyes.

"This little piggy went to market," Bridget began to sing softly into Mrs Hobson's ear, as she pushed the chair onwards. Her voice was high-pitched and girlish.

Mrs Hobson was jerked about in her seat as the chair rolled over a loose paving stone.

"This little piggy stayed at home…"

The storefront of Hobson Butchers came into view beneath the streetlamp. The door was slightly ajar.

"This little piggy had roast beef," sang Bridget as she wheeled Mrs Hobson across the store's threshold.

The smell of raw meat hit Mrs Hobson as they entered. The shop looked eerie by the soft glow of the refrigerator unit. Its hum buzzed around her ears like a swarm of flies. The glass frontage of the cold unit was slightly frosted, and behind it lay prime cuts of beef, pork, and lamb. An array of machinery stood behind the counter and nearby meat hooks jangled almost imperceptibly in the gentle breeze creeping in through the open door.

"This little piggy had none…"

Bridget stopped pushing the chair and moved to open the large metal door that led to the walk-in freezer unit. As soon as it opened, a rancid stench began to permeate the air of the shop. The freezer had been broken for nearly a week and Mr Hobson had clearly not been inside it since then. His attitude, as ever, was to leave the dirty work to someone else. Mrs Hobson suddenly felt nauseous, as the foetid air assaulted her nostrils. *Surely*, she thought, *they*

wouldn't shut me in there? With that foul old rotten meat?
She began to panic again.

Bridget wheeled Mrs Hobson through the doorway into the warm and stale walk-in unit. The latter felt herself begin to gag, as the vile odour of putrefaction became much stronger. There was very little light and Mrs Hobson struggled to see what was happening in front of her, although there was quite clearly movement.

"This little piggy went..." Bridget began and flicked the light switch.

Mrs Hobson shrieked as loudly and wildly as she was able to, a horrible, strangulated sound that echoed around the metallic walls. The light that now bathed the blood stained room revealed the malevolent old woman whom she knew all too well was due to make an appearance. The crone's eyes were glowing yellow. She stood, cleaver in hand, by a giant table. Atop this lay a dead, rotted pig. Its body had already begun the process of decay and flies buzzed around the greying, pulpy remains.

Bridget began to laugh, *"...all the way home!"*

"Now then Valerie," the old woman croaked, staring Mrs Hobson in the face. "It seems you and your husband do not understand the importance of a promise."

Mrs Hobson wished she could move her head to shake it violently. She tried to gesture with her eyes that she was sorry, that it wasn't her fault and that she didn't deserve to be here in this hideous box of mouldering death. The cleaver in the old woman's hand came down hard against the pig, slicing through flesh and bone, removing one of its trotters. She walked towards Mrs Hobson and placed the rotted trotter in the latter's paralysed left hand, uncoiling the numb fingers and locking them in place around it.

"We had an agreement. You tried to question it once before and, well, I would've thought that you and George would've learnt your lesson from that. Especially you,

Valerie."

The old crone hacked off a second stale trotter and affixed it in the clawed, petrified right hand of Mrs Hobson.

"It seems not though. Now you deny us once more your daughter. You try to fight us. Fight the will of the…" Mrs Hobson' eyes were filled with tears and, upon noticing this, the crone stopped mid-sentence. "What? Is there something wrong?"

She brought the cleaver down furiously a third time, then a fourth, a fifth and finally a sixth as the pig's head was freed from its body. Maggots began spewing from the open stump and the smell was unbearable.

"We will have her. We will have her regardless of what you say. I want you to know that," the old woman spat, edging towards her victim with the ghastly pig head clutched between her hands.

Mrs Hobson wished more than ever that she could move her head, slide her body out of the chair, run, walk, or even crawl away, somehow manage to prevent the inevitable. It was useless. All the straining and struggling accomplished was that her eyes became even mistier with tears and her pulse accelerated to an uncomfortable speed.

The crone slid the pig's head down over Mrs Hobson's, with a sickening slither, as sinews tickled across her face. The stench of the putrefying meat as it slipped down across her nose and towards her mouth made her gag immediately and she felt the burning sting of vomit discharging from her throat. She tasted strips of peeling, rancid pig flesh dripping into her mouth, mingling with the sick that she was desperately trying to spit out. As the pig's head finally engulfed her, covering her entire face, she felt the maggots crawling onto her and slipping down her skin; their warm, moist bodies finding their way into her nose, into her eyes; stinging and scrambling around within the folds of her eyelids.

"This little piggy went to market! This little piggy stayed at home! This little piggy had roast beef! This little piggy had none!" she heard Bridget screeching rapidly, like a demented cheerleader.

Mrs Hobson jerked her head to the side as violently as she could manage and a whole new slew of maggots fell from within the snout into her mouth. She knew they were crawling their way across her useless tongue, towards her throat and fought to cough them out, but it was no use. She felt their tiny bodies tumbling down her windpipe, worming their way inside her. She vomited again but felt the hot bile gliding back down her throat. It was unable to make its way out of her mouth, now filled as it was with maggots and the rapidly peeling pig flesh. She took quick breaths inwards, trying hard not to inhale the slithering creatures, tried breathing out hard but there was no room for the air to circulate. She felt her temples throb and her face becoming hot with the effort of trying to breathe.

"This little piggy went to market! This little piggy stayed at home! This little piggy had roast beef! This little piggy had none!"

Mrs Hobson began to choke fiercely as more maggots fell down her gullet, creating a complete blockage. She knew the next surge of vomit would have no means of escape at all and she felt her insides heaving and twitching. She was feebly gasping for air. The last few attempts at breathing were filled with air putrid beyond belief. These led to a seizure of furious coughing and gagging that had her rocking spasmodically in her wheelchair.

"This little piggy went to market! This little piggy stayed at home! This little piggy had roast beef! This little piggy had none!"

Bridget danced around the lifeless corpse of Mrs Hobson, with its pig's head and trotters, slumped in the wheelchair creating a surreal and grotesque tableau of death.

XVI

Peter and Jeff slipped casually out of the Bull's Head Inn without anyone really paying attention. The crowd were engaged merrily in a sing along of "Lily The Pink" and largely quite drunk by this stage.

"Oooh, we'll drink, we'll drink, we'll drink, to Lily the pink, the pink, the pink!" the pub crowd sang in deafening chorus as the brothers closed the door on the commotion, heading off into the rainy streets of Broadoak.

"I can't believe we're doing this," muttered Jeff, clutching a freshly opened can of lager he'd been stashing in his coat pocket.

"Oh, c-cc'mon, you're getting a thrill out of it, I c-c-can tell. This is the most excitement you've had in years!"

"Sad thing is, you could be right there."

Within a minute or two they were far enough away from the Bull's Head for the drunken chorus to fade into insignificance. Baker and Sons Funeral Directors was not a long walk away and they found themselves outside in no time. The building was on a fairly secluded back street, not part of the comparatively busy high road, where the brothers had seen the odd one or two passer-bys weaving their way back slightly early from the town's pubs.

"You know how to housebreak then?" Jeff asked, casually, as they stood facing one another by the front door.

"It's not hard to pic-k a loc-k-k. I got a few tips on that kind of thing in prison anyway. Basic-c shit, y'know?" Peter grinned, mischievously. Jeff wasn't sure if he was making this up or not.

"I'll keep lookout then, shall I?"

"Sure, go for it."

Jeff surveyed the dimly lit side street and sighed. The

beer had made his head fuzzy and he was descending into familiar melancholia. The street was at a slight incline and Jeff stood, watching the rainwater run downwards like a slow, tiny river flowing into the drains beneath the pavement. It reminded him briefly of his father and he tried to imagine the old man falling to his death in the Severn. It still didn't add up.

He was staring up at the windows above the shop fronts, making sure no curious eyes were peering out of them, when he heard a clicking sound followed by a yell of "oh yes!" from Peter's direction.

"You done?" he asked, but the question was already redundant as Peter had pushed open the door into the funeral parlour and was already walking inside. Jeff followed hurriedly.

The smell of formaldehyde hit them at once upon entry. Even though effort had been made to neutralise the odour with what smelt like several ill-matching air freshener sprays, the chemical stench still remained the strongest.

"Where do they keep the bodies?" Jeff asked, in a whispered voice.

"Search me, I've never been here before either."

"Shall we try down there?"

"Sure, but only if you promise to stop whispering. There's... no... one... here!" Peter shouted. It echoed slightly around the large waiting room.

"Ok, ok!"

They walked through the reception area and into a long hallway. At the end of the hallway was a wooden door that, upon being opened, revealed a staircase leading downwards. The brothers fumbled their way down. They closed the door behind them, which plunged them into pitch darkness.

"Should we switch a light on?" Jeff asked, tripping a little as he misjudged the distance between two steps.

"I think we'll have to wait 'til we get down there. I didn't want to switch any on upstairs in c-c-case anyone saw it from the street and got suspicious."

The brothers felt their way down by clinging onto the walls, which were freezing cold and unpleasantly damp. Eventually, they reached the bottom and Peter moved his hands around until he located a light switch. With an almost inaudible click, a stream of fluorescent lights spluttered to life above their heads, revealing a sterile mortuary with cream coloured walls and a black and white chequered floor. An anonymous body lay beneath a shroud on a trolley, beside a mahogany coffin. There were a number of closed metal drawers in the wall

"You think that's him?" asked Jeff, beginning to whisper again as he looked at the shrouded corpse.

"Dunno, let's check."

Peter approached the corpse and took a look at its foot. There was a small paper tag tied around its largest toe.

"Jarman, D," read Peter aloud. "It's not him."

"Jesus, it stinks in here. Smells like shit."

"It probably is shit."

"Maybe he's in one of the… drawers," suggested Jeff, trying not to think about it.

Peter walked across to the wall of drawers and began examining the names, mumbling them aloud as he went. "Davies, G! Here he is."

Jeff joined him and they both looked at one another, as if to ask if each one was sure this was the right thing to be doing. Jeff nodded imperceptibly and Peter slowly began to pull open the drawer, revealing it an inch or two at a time. The corpse inside appeared to be already dressed in a black dinner suit. As it began to show itself, Peter noticed that both hands were missing.

"Fuck-k! Look! The hands! There's no bloody hands!" cried Peter.

"Oh Jesus, oh Jesus, oh Jesus…"

"Let's get a look-k-k at his f…"

"You hear that?" hissed Jeff, interrupting and waving his hands.

There was a whistle echoing through the basement and some footsteps on the staircase. The melody of the whistling was familiar. "London Calling" by The Clash. Peter heard it and immediately plunged his head into his hands, in sheer frustration.

"God, no."

Sergeant Owen MacRae appeared at the foot of the staircase, calm and smiling. "Well, well. Got ourselves a regular Burke and Hare here, eh boys? Is this how you treat your dead down in the Smoke?"

"It was…" Jeff began, but Peter grabbed his arm, signalling for him to stop.

"Do you have a breaking and entering law down there, or is it just so common that they don't even bother?"

The brothers remained silent.

"'Cos even if somehow I couldn't bust your city arses for that, I could still have you for tampering with the bodies in here. Now get the fuck away from those drawers. I'm taking you in." He pulled out two pairs of handcuffs and grinned. "I've been waiting so fucking long for this."

XVII

As dawn rose over Broadoak, the sun shone through the clouds for the first time in days. Though the air remained chilly and bleak, the sky was blue and lit up with a low, blinding white winter sun. Mr Hobson awoke early with a feeling of dread hanging over him. He had slept fitfully and dreamt of runes and roses. The black envelope had rested on the table beside the bed, watching him ominously throughout the night.

He got up and went to the bathroom, putting off the inevitable trip to his wife's room to check on her. He suspected she would no longer be there. He knew he had had to make the choice between Valerie and Sarah last night, even though it had not been explicitly spoken. Having brushed his teeth and washed his face, Mr Hobson finally plucked up the courage to go into Valerie's room and felt nothing beyond a strange sense of emptiness as he discovered her absence. Sarah was coming out of her room at this point and Mr Hobson closed the door hurriedly. *She must not know.*

"Oh, 'ello Sarah," he said, trying weakly to smile.

"Mornin', Dad," she replied blearily. "How's Mum?"

"She's fine. Bit sleepy this morning though. Think she's going to stay in bed."

"Cool, whatever."

Sarah disappeared into the bathroom and began her morning ritual. Her eyes kept being drawn to the silver serpent ring on her finger. She had slept as badly as her father had last night, having been woken by all sorts of imaginary noises. She blamed it on the fact her thoughts were disturbed by Peter Davies and his dead father. It was probably as much due to the sheer boredom of living in Broadoak as anything else, but she was hooked on the mystery already, without even knowing precisely what it was. She only knew that Guy Davies was an alleged child molester who had evidently died a violent death and that someone was trying to cover it up. Couple that with his attractive, enigmatic and troubled son being in town and it sounded like something from a bad, but entertaining, B-Movie; the kind Sarah would always stay up late for on Friday nights.

She smiled as she pouted and admired her reflection in the mirror. She had already decided she was going to spend her Saturday at Guy Davies' funeral.

Mr Hobson, meanwhile, was preparing himself to go to work, wondering how he would be able to keep up the façade of its being a normal day when he knew his wife was missing and in the hands of the most dangerous group of people he knew. They had her. That much was certain. He had broken the pact and the cost would be blood. He wondered if they would offer him a chance to reconsider. Probably not considering this was technically his second strike.

He trudged up Wilton Road, past Baker and Sons Funeral Parlour, shielding his eyes from the brightness of the sun, wishing it would go away and not bother him while he was deep in his miserable thoughts. Eventually he reached his shop and was dismayed to find the door was unlocked and propped open. Mrs Deering was just arriving from the opposite direction.

"Good morning, dearie," she cooed. "Your door is open."

"Oh 'ello Mrs Deering. I must've left it that way. I'm getting a bit dozy in me old age, eh?"

"Ooh you cheeky young thing! Wait until you're my age!"

They both laughed but for Mr Hobson, the mirth was very forced indeed.

"I was hoping to get one of your pies, dear, if I'm not too early?"

Mr Hobson stuttered. He was averse to letting anyone into the shop until he had seen what was in there for himself. He already had a horrible premonition of what it may be.

"I'm sorry, love, I 'aven't 'ad chance to make any up yet. You'll 'ave to come back later when I has."

"Not a problem, dear, I know how it is. I'll pop by at lunchtime ok?"

"Ta, love. I'll see you later. Don't forget, I close at one on Saturdays though."

"I won't, dearie."

As Mrs Deering hobbled off down the street, Mr Hobson stepped into his shop and immediately closed the door behind him, breathing heavily and nervously. The shop seemed to be in reasonable condition and, on first glance, nothing had been stolen or broken. The metal door to the walk-in freezer seemed to be staring at him, mocking him and begging him to open it. He walked slowly towards it and turned the handle.

Inside, the walls were covered in blood, more red than grey. The room was full of flies and little pools of maggots were crawling on the floor. The stench of blood, shit and putrefaction was overwhelming and Mr Hobson fought back the urge to vomit. In the middle of the room was his wife, Valerie Hobson, locked in deathly stillness, sat in her wheelchair, a pig trotter in each hand and a vile, still dripping pig's head on her own.

He held his head in his hands at the sight and began to sob.

"Oh Valerie, I'm so sorry," he whispered, but he knew what he had to do.

He went back into the store, strapped on his apron and

removed the electric carving knife from beneath the counter. Returning to the freezer, he plugged it in and walked over to his wife. Taking a deep breath and biting his lower lip, he switched on the knife and slowly brought it down onto his wife's shoulder, slicing through the flesh. It struggled a little with the bone but was designed for carving through it so eventually, with a sickly splutter and a little spray of marrow, cut clean through.

Once each arm had been removed, Mr Hobson repeated the process with his wife's legs, removing them and cutting each one in half. Valerie's blood was all over his apron and hands as he took the trunk of her body and sliced it in half, peeling open the ribcage with his fingers and taking out the slippery viscera inside.

Eventually he came to the head, which he calmly sliced off and stripped of its porcine mask. Valerie's eyes were white, having rolled back and there was dried vomit all over her face. He closed the eyes and wept as he used the knife to split her skull in half. He knew it was imperative that even if her remains were found, she should not be able to be identified.

Covered in blood and sinew, he put each individual part of his wife's carcass into separate black bags and dragged them into the kitchen. He lit the flame beneath the large metal pot used for boiling stews and pie mix and, when the water inside was bubbling, put each of the body parts into it, one by one. Later, when the flesh had melted and the bones were clean, he would bag them up once more and bury them in the garden. But for now, he simply sat and wept.

XVIII

Jeff and Peter had to share a cell in the local gaol. They spoke no words to one another throughout the night and both went to sleep in surly moods, almost as soon as the cell door was locked. In the morning, sunlight filtering through the bars woke both of them up. Peter was the first to speak.

"You up yet?" he asked.

"No. Fuck off," Jeff grumbled in response.

"Look-k. I fuc-k-ked up ok-k? I'm sorry. Can we not dwell on it? I thought maybe if we slept on it…"

"…then what? I'd forget I now have a criminal record. God only knows what my boss'd say if he heard about this. I take a few days off to go to my Dad's funeral and return to London with a criminal record for trying to interfere with his corpse! I'd be bloody fired in a shot. Probably sectioned too!"

"Oh don't be such a bloody drama queen. We don't even know what the charge is yet. Fuck-king MacRae wasn't really in a patient enough mood to ex-xplain just what was going on."

There was a clicking and the echo of a bang from further down the corridor, followed by several pairs of footsteps. As the door to the cell rattled and opened, Owen MacRae and Jenny Davies walked in to join the brothers. Owen was dressed in a black suit, instead of his uniform, and Jenny was also wearing a mourning outfit.

"Speak of the Devil…" muttered Peter.

"Morning, brothers," beamed MacRae viciously, his spiked hair shining greasily in the stark sunlight.

Jenny glared at Peter and Jeff, who both sat up on their cell beds. "What the fuck were you doing?"

"Jenny, please. I can't really…" began Jeff, looking at the ground.

"You know what? I don't even want to know. I don't even care. You two are so beyond fucked. I don't know what happened to you, Jeff. I thought you were the normal one. The one who wasn't a complete fucking screw-up."

"It was my idea," murmured Peter. "Jeff was just drunk, so he went along with it."

"Yes, I understand he was," spat Jenny. "Owen told me last night the pair of you stank pretty strongly of beer when he picked you up at the funeral home, hands all over Dad's dead body!"

"We were looking for something," said Peter, bluntly.

"Oh?" MacRae's interest was suddenly piqued.

"We didn't find it."

"Shame."

"Yeah."

"You're lucky anyway," said Jenny, fumbling in her handbag for a cigarette. "Mr Baker isn't pressing charges against you. He reckons you were acting under the influence of undue stress and grief."

"So does that mean we can go?" Jeff piped up.

"He wants you to replace his lock. You bust it when you broke in."

"No problem. I'll give him the money later. Can we go?"

"Yeah. I can't keep you any longer I'm afraid," said MacRae. "But Baker told me to pass on a message to you both. He said that next time you want a hot date for a Friday night, you're gonna have to pay like everyone else does. He's got some fresher ones than your Dad, too, he says."

Peter sprung up from the bed but Jeff caught him and pulled him back in time.

"Hoo, woah there, London. Want to add assaulting a police officer to your list of offences? I think your parole officer would already be pretty interested to hear what you've been up to but your sister here talked me out of telling him, ok? So go a little easy."

Peter just glared.

In a matter of minutes, their belongings had been returned and the brothers stood outside. Owen and Jenny had waited indoors, clearly not wanting to accompany Pete and Jeff to the funeral.

"What's the time?" asked Jeff. "My 'phone ran out of battery and I don't have a watch."

"It's half nine," replied Peter. "Funeral's in an hour."

They looked at each other for a second too long and Peter burst out laughing. Jeff joined in and before long both had tears streaming down their faces.

"In hindsight," spluttered Jeff, "that was pretty funny."

"Like I said to you last night, it's probably the most excitement you've had in years."

"Oh ha ha. But the look on MacRae's face when he had to let us go! Classic!"

"Yeah, I must buy old Bak-k-ker a pint sometime soon."

They regained composure as they began walking back down Cinderford Road to the town centre.

"Of c-c-course, there's still the issue of Dad's hands."

Jeff sighed. "Yeah, I'll give it to you. That is pretty strange. I noticed you kept it secret from MacRae though?"

"Yeah, well, as if he's going to help us."

"Everything else aside though, he *is* the police. He probably already knows about it. I dunno. I don't know what happens when police are investigating things. How much they withhold from the public."

"From the family?"

"I guess. I don't know."

"Do you think Jenny knows his hands are missing?"

"I have no idea. I'm getting a really weird feeling from Jen these last couple of days. As if she's blocking me out on purpose, as if she knows something and doesn't want me to

94

find out. So maybe."

"Maybe that's it? Maybe there's something the police know that the public don't. Mac-c-cRae told Jenny bec-cause they're going out? But it's got to be kept under wraps for whatever reason while they solve the case?"

Jeff laughed. "I have no idea. My knowledge of police procedures stretches about as far as watching 'The Bill'."

"Yeah? Mine's more like 'The Thin Blue Line'."

"So we should probably stop speculating."

"It doesn't make sense though. Surely if a serious investigation was going on, they wouldn't be allowed to bury him today? It'd be like destroying evidence or something."

"Evidence of what though? We still don't actually have a clue what happened."

"You know what? Fuck-k-k it. Funeral's in less than an hour, the old man'll be done with and that's that. Let's just get back-k to London tomorrow and on with our lives. I'm so sick-k of death of this stupid family and this stupid town." Peter grinned. "Sod 'em."

"I never thought I'd say this but I think I've had enough excitement for one weekend too. I think going back to boring old London is probably a good idea. I swear we're losing it being up here. We broke into a bloody funeral home last night, for Christ's sake!"

"Don't get me wrong, I still think it's weird, what's happening. I just don't *c-care* any more."

"Come on, let's get dressed and get this thing over with."

XIX

Sarah Hobson arrived at Broadoak cemetery a little early. She wore a plain black blouse and black school trousers, the most appropriate ensemble she could find for the occasion. Whilst waiting for anyone else familiar to arrive, she rolled a joint and wandered off to smoke it behind a tall headstone carved into the shape of an angel.

She smoked quickly and by the time she'd finished, she felt a mellow buzz all over her, a strange sense of elation. The bitter air of the cemetery didn't bother her and the sunlight in her eyes felt enlightening not obtrusive. From the corner of her vision, she noticed a small cluster of people beginning to filter into the small Victorian church near the gates of the cemetery. She followed suit and slid onto a pew inside.

The congregation was small. Ethyl, Mr Taverner, Jenny and Seargeant MacRae were already sat in the front row. Peter was nowhere to be seen yet, so Sarah shifted uncomfortably on her pew, wishing she'd sat closer to the back. Ethyl from the flower shop turned around and smiled at Sarah. "Lovely to see you, Sarah," she whispered.

Sarah's pulse was racing now, as the buzz from the marijuana began to dissipate. She hoped no one would talk to her or ask her why she was there. She would not know how to explain it. Five excruciating minutes passed, as she sat uncomfortably on the pew listening to a cassette tape playing moribund organ music through an expensive pair of new speakers that had replaced the organist. The vicar shuffled back and forth at the front of the church besides a large oak coffin, looking simultaneously nervous and bored. The church itself was sparsely decorated, with very little of the usual ornate religious paraphernalia one normally sees in such places. It felt soulless and cold.

The doors opened, to reveal Peter and Jeff entering the church. Jeff was dressed solemnly in black and Peter wore a navy blue suit with matching tie. Sarah fought back an urge to giggle, she was so relieved. She turned to face Peter and smiled at him, receiving a slightly quizzical look and an arched eyebrow in return. The two brothers sat down in the front pew and the ceremony began. Sarah had never attended a funeral before in her life so was not entirely sure if this ranked as a good or a bad one. The vicar recited monotonously from a bible and spoke about Guy Davies being in a "better place" now. Sarah's attention wavered after the first hymn was sang and she began to more closely examine the attendees of the funeral.

She noticed that MacRae looked edgy, glancing around the church innumerable times as if expecting something terrible to happen. She watched the hands of Jenny Davies that were twitching, fingers flicking one another as if craving a cigarette. She wondered what life must be like between the two of them. MacRae was renowned throughout the town for being a nasty, violent piece of work and Sarah wondered if poor Jenny had ever been on the receiving end of his temper.

Mr Taverner was standing upright, squirming a little in a black suit a size too small for him. His hulking frame seemed ready to burst out of the fabric. Little Ethyl, next to him, appeared like a dwarf by comparison. She stood at half his height and was concentrating intently on the words of the vicar.

The two brothers at the front seemed embarrassed to be there, scratching their heads and shuffling a little on each foot, when everyone stood for the hymns.

No one cried.

When the time came to carry the coffin out into the churchyard, Jeff, Peter, Taverner and MacRae acted as pallbearers. Sarah noticed a good many filthy looks exchanged between Peter and MacRae as the four of them solemnly hauled the body of Guy Davies out into the windy November morning, followed by Ethyl, Sarah and the vicar. A surly young man with a harelip and a shovel watched on.

The box was lowered carefully into a hole that had been dug in the earth. The headstone was not yet present. The vicar began to intone a psalm that blurred into meaningless babble before reaching Sarah's ears. Jenny placed a wreath on the coffin, atop a golden cross that had been affixed to the box. Everyone else took turns to toss a handful of dirt into the grave and, when the service was complete, the brothers thanked the vicar and everyone headed off towards the cemetery gates, a sense of deflation and anti-climax hanging over their heads.

"I didn't realise you knew him," drawled Peter as Sarah caught up with him and appeared alongside.

"I didn't. I came to see you." Sarah left an intentional pause for this shock revelation to sink in. It worked. Peter looked suddenly disarmed. "You seemed a bit upset last night when I told you about the hand and all that shite. I just wanted to check you were ok. I'm sorry if…"

"Don't be, it's fine. I believe you about the hand."

"Yeah?"

"Yeah. Thanks for letting me know."

"Err… Are you sure you still don't want the ring back?"

"No thanks. As I said, k-k-eep it."

They walked another few steps before Peter leaned in a little to her and lowered his voice. "Look, it's nice of you to c-c-c-come today but it's probably best if you go now. If people see us talking, they're bound to think-k the worst."

Sarah felt her heart sink. She asked, "what?" but she knew full well what he meant.

"I'm sorry. I really do appreciate you being here

though."

"Whatever." Sarah began to walk quickly away.

"Wait!" hissed Peter, a little uncertainly. "I'll... I'll meet you later if you want to talk-k?"

"Where?" she asked, a little too quickly, betraying her eagerness.

"Outside the Bull's Head? At seven, yeah?"

"Ok!" Sarah smiled and walked away, trying not to think too hard about what was happening. She knew she was playing dangerously because, as meek and charming as Peter appeared, he was still technically a convicted sex offender. Secretly, she thought to herself with some shame, she was pleased because she knew already he would not refuse her advances for being too young. She immediately tried to steer her mind away from these wicked thoughts and onto inane trivia. It didn't work.

"What the shite is wrong with me?" she muttered to herself, wandering off down Conker Lane and kicking a pinecone onto the grass. "Why am I even thinking like this?"

She came upon a stile on a gate that linked Conker Lane to the town centre and sat on it for awhile, rolling herself another joint and wondering if perhaps she was smoking too much lately. Everything seemed so unpleasant right now though. Dad was going through something at home and she wished he felt he could talk about it with her. But communication was never a strong point for the Hobson family. They were content to spend a few minutes a night making small talk over dinner but, this aside, they were more or less strangers to one another.

Sarah stuck her headphones on and zoned out for an hour, happily listening to the music, smoking and watching the golden brown leaves dancing in the wind down Conker Lane. It was only when her fingertips started to become numb from the cold that she returned home. There was a plain black envelope on the doormat that had been pushed through the letterbox and obscured beneath a pile of junk mail promoting special offers from a new supermarket opening soon in Gloucester. Sarah did not stop to look at it as she leisurely walked upstairs to her bedroom.

XX

"What the Hell was that all about?" asked Jeff in an agitated whisper, catching up with his brother as they walked out of Broadoak cemetery together.

"What was all what about?"

"Sarah Hobson. What was she doing here today?"

"I dunno. She c-c-came of her own free will. I didn't know she was going to be here. I didn't ask her, if that's what you mean."

"So what were you just talking about with her?"

"I dunno. She wanted to speak-k to me about something. I'm going to meet her later."

"You're going to meet her?" Jeff looked mortified.

"Yeah? And?"

"She's fourteen, Peter."

"What's your point?"

Jeff put his hand against his forehead and squeezed his temples, taking a deep breath. "It's funny, you know? Sometimes I forget."

"Forget what?"

"I dunno. I get talking with this guy, this pretty funny, normal, even nice guy who's my brother and I forget all about everything else. Then something like this happens."

"Like what? Jesus, Jeff, stop being such a bloody drama queen and tell me what's wrong."

"You're having a meeting tonight with a fourteen year old girl. You have a conviction for exposing yourself to a twelve year old one! Do you not see where I'm going? Do you really want me to spell it out for you?"

"Woah, hang on. I don't think about Sarah like that. She's just a bit of a c-c-confused k-kid. She wants to talk-k to me about something. I'm c-c-c-curious. She's about the most interesting person I'm lik-kely to find in Broadoak-k to tal-

101

k-k to unless I fancy a game of dominoes and a chat about what type of bait to use while fishing in the brook-k!"

"I'm sorry but, come on, you can't blame me for thinking the worst."

"C-c-can't I?" Peter exploded. "Did you ever once stop to ask-k about anything that happened three years ago? Did you ever even think-k about it? It's not something I'm proud of. I don't walk-k round yelling about it. I was going through some serious shit. I didn't have a single person in the fuck-king world to talk to about it. Everything just got out of control. To be honest, I can barely even remember the moment it happened. I don't even remember exactly what I did. I just remember something tak-king over, just these… urges that I c-c-couldn't fight any more."

"Peter. No matter what you tell me now, I'm never going to understand why you did what you did…" Jeff began, shaking his head. "Never."

"I'm not ask-king you to. But really. Is it so hard? Not if you really think-k hard about yourself. You just don't want to because you're terrified about what might be inside you. You can't face up to that beast. Well, I have. I've faced it, I tried to fight it and I lost. But now I'm fighting again and this time, I might just be winning. I see a therapist twice a week-k. I have my parole officer. I've got a little job. I'm really trying to straighten my life out."

"I'm sorry," Jeff mumbled. "I just… I just don't know how to deal with any of this."

"You know something?" Peter asked, grinning at his brother, his eyes brightening a little. "Nor do I."

Jeff laughed weakly. "I don't mean to be so judgemental. I just… I feel so weird right now."

"It's ok-k. Honestly. We're both on edge."

"Fancy a pint?"

"Nah, no thank-ks. I'm going to get some rest for a bit. Might see you later if I'm up."

"Alright. Take care, ok."

"I will."

They patted one another on the shoulders and walked away in separate directions.

XXI

"No pies at all, dear?" asked Mrs Deering, her forehead crumpling into a wrinkled tangle of distress upon hearing the news.

"I'm sorry, love, we've got a problem with the vat I use for the pie mix. Can't 'elp you at all today."

"Oh, well, in that case, I'd better just get a rasher or two of your smoked Danish. I'll make myself a sandwich."

"Not a problem, Mrs Deering. Let me assure you there'll be pies again this time next week. Your first one's on the 'ouse for your troubles."

"Oh Mr Hobson, you're too kind, dearie."

"Well, I 'as to keep the customers 'appy, don't I?" he replied, smiling and handing her a polythene bag full of bacon, sealed with a price label. "Ninety-five pence, thanking you."

Mrs Deering paid up and left the shop. As soon as the door closed, Mr Hobson walked towards it and flipped over the cardboard sign hanging in it. 'CLOSED'. He wandered back into the kitchen area and began sobbing again, as he looked upon the metal vat, bubbling away, stripping the flesh from the bones of his dismembered wife and boiling her innards. The kitchen now smelt rank and unusual, an aroma not unlike boiled meat, mixing with something altogether less preferable. He washed his hands in the cold ceramic sink, watching the pinkish mix of blood and water spiral down the plughole. He peered into the bubbling vat of grue. Some of the smaller bones were floating on top of the crimson water, like soap in a bathtub.

There was a clanking sound followed by the horrific squeal of metal on metal, which prompted Hobson to spin around. Standing in the doorway of the kitchen was the half-wit girl, Bridget. She was running a meat hook along the metal wall, creating that awful noise. She was wearing a black, toga-like sack and a wreath of flowers upon her head.

"For the love of God, woman, stop!" cried Hobson, covering his ears with his dripping hands.

Bridget laughed, but dropped the meat hook nonetheless.

"What is it you want? Haven't you lot 'ad enough yet?" he pleaded.

"Do you like my flowers?" asked Bridget.

Hobson remained silent.

"I stole them from Guy Davies. Took them from his grave. You know they buried him today?"

"God save the poor sod's soul."

"They put a golden cross on his coffin. Just for show, you know? I took that too. Frigged myself with it. Got so excited, I pissed myself too. All over his grave."

"Look you," snarled Hobson. "After all I've bloody been through today, it'll take more than these stupid scare tactics to get me hackles up."

"I like the smell of your pie mix today," chimed the girl, in a singsong voice. "May I try some?"

Mr Hobson stared aghast at the girl at she scooped out a trickling handful of viscera and squeezed it, the boiling juices and deep red gristle oozing through her fingers. With a sudden movement, she stuffed it into her mouth and began chewing furiously, blood dripping down her chin. Her eyes were glowing bright yellow as she giggled and licked her lips, fishing her hand into the boiling vat to pull out a long, white bone.

She licked the bone seductively. Her unnatural forked tongue slid out of her mouth and coiled itself around the bone. She moved it in and out of her mouth until Hobson was so sickened, he was forced to turn away.

"Oh, for pity's sake, stop!"

Bridget burst into hysterical laughter and tossed the bone away. "Did you get our letter?" she asked.

"No?"

"Oh dear. You must have left too early this morning for the postie."

Hobson felt a tingling in his veins, as his blood ran cold with fear. "A… black note?"

"I'm afraid so."

He knew the meaning of a black note all too well. Someone had to die. Someone else.

"You know what I used to love when I was a little girl?" asked Bridget, idly picking flowers from the wreath on her head. "Fireworks! Bang! Bang! Bang!"

Hobson just stared at his feet, wishing the girl would stop prolonging the inevitable.

"I used to love the bonfires, the sparklers, the guy. My auntie used to take me to the display in the park every year. It's tonight, you know?"

"I know."

"How would you like to come with me? Be my date?" She twisted her neck and slid, snake-like, out of her black sack, now standing naked before him in the dim glow of the kitchen lights.

He stuttered and his eyes began welling with tears. Before he could say a word, she was upon him, smothering him with the black sack. He struggled and squirmed briefly but it was in vain. Her inhuman body had snaked around him and was crushing the air out of him like a boa constrictor. He lapsed into unconsciousness.

XXII

After the funeral, Peter returned to his room at the Bull's Head Inn to catch up on the sleep he had lost, tossing and turning in the prison cell bed. It had reminded him all too much of the awful two years spent in similar conditions and he had barely slept a wink. As he was falling into uneasily pleasant dreams about Sarah Hobson, his brother was sitting down in the Old Crown with a mug of Mrs Taverner's mulled wine, on the house. Ethyl was enjoying a glass of sherry at the same table, sharing a memory of Guy Davies.

"And then your father said to me 'but Ethyl, you're the oldest person I know!' I couldn't help but laugh!" she responded.

Jeff laughed politely but his thoughts were elsewhere. It was nice to spend time with Ethyl, who was always gregarious and kind, but he really was just counting the hours until he could leave Broadoak and return to London. The town was draining him of energy and after the catharsis of seeing his father laid in the ground, he felt he had hit rock bottom. He had forgotten how irritating the small town life could be. Even the fact that in the deserted silence of the Old Crown, Ethyl and Jeff's conversation could be heard by all the other customers in the pub, bothered him intensely right now. That said, there was barely a soul in sight who'd care.

The only other customers were two older men in fleecy pullovers, sat in the corner playing a game of shove ha'penny, and smoking cigars.

"What are you thinking about, Jeffrey?" asked Ethyl, reaching her hand across the table to him.

"Oh, nothing. Just I dunno. It's all a bit weird. Coming back here, seeing Dad buried, it's all kinda flown by in a bit of a whirlwind. I'm heading back to London tomorrow and then I'll be back at work on Monday as if nothing's happened. It's weird to think that. As if the whole thing's been a dream."

"I understand."

"That business with Dad in the newspapers too, that's just horrible. I don't know what to think. All that stuff with the little girl."

"Oh, don't you worry about that. It'll blow over as quickly as all these silly rumours do. They'll find that girl soon enough and no one will even remember your father had anything to do with it."

"Yeah. You're right. I hope anyway. It just feels so wrong."

"You know you're always welcome here, Jeffrey. Even with your father dead, you'll always have a good friend in me," she smiled tenderly.

"I know. I know. Thank you."

"So what are you doing tonight, for your last night in Broadoak? Are you coming to the fireworks display in the park?"

"Heh. Yeah, may as well. I haven't been to that since I was about five."

"Oh, it should be great. I enjoy a good bonfire night. It gets a little noisy for my old ears, what with all the bangers, but I do love twirling a sparkler around!"

Jeff smiled and leant back in his chair, taking a healthy gulp of the mulled wine. The taste reminded him of bygone winters. He idly wondered what he was going to do this Christmas. Maybe he should spend it with Ethyl in Broadoak? The alternative was being alone in London, or perhaps just asking around the office, seeing if there are any other lonely souls with nothing better to do than maybe grab a pub lunch with a colleague. Of course, there was the other option. He and Peter could spend Christmas together in London. But that was too strange still. As much as he had been getting on with his brother for the past few days, it still niggled in the back of his mind about the conviction. He still felt uncomfortable and confused when sat opposite from this man whom he could never hope to understand, even though they shared the same blood. There was an air of guilt hanging over him for his earlier outburst at Peter but he still felt it was too difficult to understand what on Earth could've driven such a rational man to act the way he did. Jeff felt a shiver down his spine as he recalled the rumours about his father, too.

The door creaked open and a young man walked in, his hands and face muddy and a shovel in his hand. Jeff recognised him as the surly gravedigger who had been at the cemetery when his father was being buried.

"Afternoon, Selwyn," hollered Taverner as the boy approached the bar.

"Hello, squire!" The boy spoke with a Welsh accent. "I'll have a pint of the Adnams, please."

Taverner began pouring the beer. "This'uns on the house, lad. You just buried a good friend o'mine."

"Cheers, matey."

Selwyn took his pint and milled around by the fruit machine situated by the gents' toilet. Jeff nodded politely and raised his glass in the boy's direction.

"'Scuse me, Ethyl," said Jeff, getting up and making for the lavatories. Just as he was reaching the door, Selwyn headed towards a table and bumped into Jeff, accidentally spilling a few drops of his beer.

"Oh, I'm sorry mate," said Jeff, wiping the spillage from his coat. "I didn't know you were moving this way!"

"It's no bother, so it isn't," replied Selwyn. "Don't worry about it." He extended his hand to Jeff's and shook it. Jeff was apprehensive at first about this overenthusiastic tactility but soon realised that the boy was pressing a screwed up scrap of paper into the palm of his hand. Selwyn's eyes met Jeff's with a look of burning intensity as he lowered them, as if pointing to the paper. "You just take care now, boyo," he said to Jeff, patting him on the shoulder and moving away.

"Sure, sure," Jeff said, as casually as he could manage. As soon as he got into the toilets, he unscrewed the piece of paper in his hand and read the note upon it.

"MEET ME BY YOUR FATHER'S GRAVE AT MIDNIGHT TONIGHT. BE THERE. YOUR LIFE DEPENDS ON IT. DO NOT TELL A SOUL. NO ONE. IT IS NOT SAFE IF YOU DO."

Jeff almost laughed aloud at the pomposity of the note. This was ridiculous, almost like something out of an old Sherlock Holmes story. *The game's afoot, Watson!* But there was an unnameable feeling he had inside that told him to heed the note. That look in the gravedigger's eyes had been fierce and deadly serious. Considering that last night he had broken into a funeral home to illegally examine the corpse of his father, meeting a gravedigger for an after-hours chat in the local cemetery seemed positively tame by comparison, so he decided to go through with it.

The only question was whether or not to tell Peter. The note would not permit it, but Jeff knew that if anything significant were revealed, Peter would be furious that he had not been there to learn about it. But rules were rules, Jeff thought, vowing not to tell anyone and secretly enjoying the odd thrill of this bizarre mystery. It gave him something to look forward to prior to the drive down to London. Between that and the firework display in the park, Jeff had a feeling that tonight might not turn out to be so drab after all.

XXIII

Peter had sat in the bar of the Bull's Head Inn for the past hour, sipping a half-pint of home-made scrumpy. It was a bitter and potent brew that made him feel slightly queasy, which wasn't helped by his sense of confusion and nerves over meeting Sarah tonight. He'd been quite happy to have an outburst at Jeff for being judgemental at the cemetery but deep down he knew that controlling the urges inside him would prove harder than ever. Especially now it was obvious that Sarah was interested in him. Even if it was just a teenage crush she had, and he knew better than to exploit it, the stirrings he felt within him when he saw her were becoming increasingly difficult to ignore. Maybe Jeff was right. *Of course Jeff was right.*

Peter felt ashamed, dirty. He wished he could be anywhere else. In London it was so much easier to hide away behind closed doors and disappear. People ignored you on the streets of London, he thought to himself. If Sarah Hobson was your typical fourteen-year-old London girl, she would not have even so much as glanced at him, nor given him the time of day. Her prospects would be so open, her eyes filled with so many pretty teen boys with explosive hormones, an aging cripple like Peter would fade into insignificance. In the small towns, it was different. There was really nothing better on offer, as proven when Peter looked around the Bull's Head bar.

A group of young farmer's lads were sat in a huddle in the corner, shouting and swearing, making loud jokes comparing their girlfriends to various types of livestock. Slumped over the bar was old man Crowthers, the town's most notorious drunk for as long as Peter could remember. He was asleep and dribbling a little, his head resting on a Brew IX drip tray. Mrs Deering from the sweet shop was sipping on a gin and tonic in another corner, chatting away with Piper, the newsagent. She occasionally glanced up from her conversation to cast a scornful glare at Peter. She had never liked him. Mr Piper stood up and approached the bar. Peter nodded and smiled as politely as he could.

"How're things then, Davies?" enquired Piper. He was a typical English gentleman, an anachronism. He always referred to everyone by their last name, tried to keep a stiff upper lip and a neutral opinion at all times, never wishing to offend or provoke. His thick, silvery moustache seemed to shiver as he spoke.

"Oh, y'know," replied Peter. "Things are fine I suppose. How're you?"

"Very well thank you. Mustn't grumble anyway. That's what my wife always used to say."

"Oh, how's your son doing? He must be getting big nowadays."

"Yes, he's fourteen now. He's fine. Just has a spot of the flu at the moment, hasn't been at school the last few days." Mr Piper's eyes seemed to dart down to the floor as he said this. Peter had no idea, nor did he particularly care, what the other was hiding but it was quite obvious from the body language that something was amiss.

"Hope he gets well soon."

"Thank you. My condolences about your father."

Peter raised his glass. "Cheers."

The barman appeared at that point and cut the conversation short by taking Piper's order of another gin and tonic and a pint of brown and mild. Peter glanced at his watch. It was seven'o'clock. He drained the glass of sour scrumpy and walked outside into the coldness of the evening. The air felt damp and heavy again. A particularly savage wind blowed through it. A storm was inevitably on the horizon for the next day.

He stood outside the Bull's Head, specifically edging away from the orange glow of a nearby streetlight. He thought it strange that there were so many little dark crevices you could drop into when in Broadoak. On London streets there was scarcely a place to stand where you wouldn't be bathed in the endless rows of streetlights or the blaring neon from some alleyway dive. It was from his hideaway in the darkness that he spotted Sarah Hobson walking up the road towards him. She was dressed in a long black dreadnought coat and a black woollen hat. He stepped back into the streetlight and she smiled to see him.

"Hiya," she said, quietly.

"Hey. Wanna go for a walk? It's probably not a good idea to stay around here. There's at least one person in the bar who I'd rather didn't see us together."

"Sure, where you wanna go?"

"I dunno. C-c-onk-k-k-ker Lane?"

"Easy for you to say," joked Sarah. "But nah, that leads up to the park, there'll be tons of people there all going up there for that firework shite."

"Ah yeah, good point."

"How about the river?"

"Alright, sure."

They began walking briskly down the street towards the river. The wind bit at their skin and howled around their ears. It was definitely building up to something stronger.

"Jesus, it's c-c-c-cold," remarked Peter.

"I'll say it's c-c-cold!"

"Hey, are you tak-king the piss out of me?"

"No, I'm just f-f-f-freezing!"

They both laughed a little. "My teeth are chattering," mused Peter. They could see the tops of the copper beech trees swaying off in the distance as they approached the path that led to the riverbank.

"Hey look, I don't think my dad's in tonight," said Sarah, as she stopped walking all of a sudden. "He didn't come home from work today so I guess he's gone straight to the fireworks thing. He normally sells sausages and pork barms in the park. He'll be out all night. We could go there to talk. I don't even think I could spark up in this wind."

Peter wasn't sure he trusted himself alone with Sarah behind closed doors. His heart began beating at double speed as his mind reeled off a litany of doubts. "Sure, sounds great," he said, almost involuntarily.

The two of them turned around and headed off towards the empty Hobson house.

"You like to smok-ke then?" Peter asked, with a nervy grin.

"God yeah, it's the only thing keeps me calm."

"You get that tense?"

"Wouldn't you? Living in Broadoak? This place is a fucking shitehole. I hate it. People just don't leave you alone, they're always on your back about some shite or other. I don't know why they get worked up, it's not like anything'll ever happen or change, no matter who does what. This place is so stuck up itself."

"Wow. You really don't lik-ke it here at all." "That's why I like to smoke. Just clears my head of all this horse-shite for a bit. Just like to listen to music and chill out, y'know?"

"Yeah, I know. What k-kind of music you into then?"

"Oh, you'll find out. I'll play you some," she grinned naughtily and he felt his heart skip again. He knew he would not be strong enough to resist if she made a move towards him. He tried wishing she wouldn't, but deep down knew that there was very little he wanted more.

They soon reached the house and she put her finger to her mouth. "Shhhh," she whispered. "I need to go check on my mum."

"Your mum?"

"Yeah, don't worry about her. She'll be in her room and she won't even know you're here."

Sarah let herself in and tiptoed up the stairs to her mother's room, leaving Peter waiting in the unlit murk of the living room. He stared at the red standby light on the television, waiting for Sarah to return.

"It's fucked up," she observed, walking back downstairs.

"What is?"

"She's not there. I guess Dad must've taken her to the bonfire. Weird."

"She's in a wheelchair isn't she, your mum?"

"Yeah, she's a quadriplegic. Can't move her arms or legs or nothin'. Had a stroke when I was three."

"I'm sorry." Peter always felt awkward expressing condolences to people. He was bad with empathy and always felt insincere.

"Don't worry. I'm kinda glad she's not here to be honest. At least it means we can smoke in the lounge."

Sarah pulled a polythene bag and some rolling papers from her rucksack and laid them out on the table. Peter smiled, as he watched her roll up a joint with notable finesse.

XXIV

Mr Hobson awoke in darkness, short of breath. He was baking hot all around, his last recollection being the naked Bridget leaping on him and wrapping him in the sack. His warm breath seemed to reflect from the scrappy fabric of the sack, bouncing back onto his face, sickly and sour. He felt ill and pushed out with his hands. He soon realised he was unable to move them. They were tied quite tightly to his sides. There was some kind of thick, rough rope wrapped all the way around his midriff that was pinning his arms down and creating an uncomfortable pain in his belly as it dug right into the flesh. He attempted to kick out but there were more ropes tied around his knees and ankles, binding his legs tightly together.

"'Ello?" he shouted but the words sounded dull and muffled even inside the sack. He was certain no one outside could hear him.

He attempted to squirm around but there was something hard like a giant plank of wood that was tied stiffly to his back. He jerked back and forth but the plank would not move. He realised he was tied to some kind of stake.

He strained his ears and could make out through the fabric the sound of voices. Lots of people were talking and laughing around him. They sounded somehow distant. He could swear he heard high-pitched voices, the voices of children. As his ears adjusted to the new surroundings and the cacophony of the shrieking wind rustling the sack's fabric died down, he could make out words, phrases, conversations.

"You're not getting a sparkler, Megan, you're too young. Mummy will buy one and you can watch her."

"My favourite is the Catherine Wheel!"

"Get yer roasted chestnuts! 20p a bag!

"Penny for the guy! Penny for the guy!"

Penny for the guy? Suddenly, Hobson realised where he was and screamed for his life. "NO! NO! NO!" he shouted, frantically, praying that someone would hear him as he impotently tried to kick his legs out.

There was a splashing sound from some distance below him and the smell of paraffin wafted upwards towards his nostrils. He wriggled and screamed some more but realised his efforts were futile. He had made his choice and now he was paying for it. He only hoped that death would be the last of it and that he wouldn't be interfered with or put through any further degradation after his earthly end.

The roar of fire echoed in his ears as he felt his lower body heat up slowly. Initially it was a faintly unpleasant warmth but it soon became an intense sting, then a searing sensation as his feet caught fire. He could see the fire now as the flames licked their way through the black sack, lapping at his flesh and melting through it, charring the bone beneath.

He looked down to see his legs were bubbling and blistering, the skin moving up and down, then bursting as blood and pus poured down into the flames below, leaving gaping wounds of red behind. As the flame raised higher, the unbearable stinging spread across his body and he felt the hairs on his face begin to disintegrate. The orange glow of the fire and the red of the blood that was pouring down his face turned to black as he heard a sickeningly moist popping sound and his eyes exploded. He felt the boiling liquid that remained slickly trickle down his face like egg whites. He screamed once more in vain, his ears filled with the rumbling of the fire, the crackle of his own sizzling flesh and the oozing of blood from his scorched scalp. His mouth was full of flame. His tonsils melted and dripped down his throat. He was choking on smoke and flesh. The sack was in tatters and he felt the wooden stake behind him was starting to wither and collapse from the heat.

He stopped shrieking as he felt the skin around his lips drip off down his chin towards the rumpled carpet of crimson ruin that was once his chest. The wood behind him gave way and his body fell face down into the very heart of the flames, to be consumed entirely.

* * *

Jeff had arrived at the bonfire with Ethyl, who had brought several sparklers with her. They had both lit one and were busy twirling them around, spelling out words in the nighttime air, waiting for the bonfire to start. The park was extremely busy and the vast majority of Broadoak's modest population had made an appearance there. The fireworks display, organised by the local Lions Club, was always a highlight of the town's social calendar.

It was seven thirty. Jeff and Ethyl moved towards the crowd who were huddled around a large pile of boxes and timber that had been stacked in the middle of the park behind several wooden stakes. There were signs posted on each stake that read "KEEP OUT" and, atop the gigantic mound of wood and cardboard, there was a flaccid looking guy, draped in a black sack.

"They've got a big guy this year, haven't they Jeffrey?" remarked Ethyl as they craned for a better view.

"Yeah, bet he'll go up well," Jeff said. He was quite excited by the party atmosphere and nostalgic reverie that the bonfire display was awakening with him.

Mrs Deering and Mr Piper were stood nearby, clearly a little tipsy. They waved to Jeff who walked over to say "hello" and remark on the size of the guy.

"Ooh, dear, you are right, it is a big'un!" she cooed, winking at Mr Piper, who let out a small cough under his breath.

Just then, a cheer rose up through the crowd followed by clapping and laughing as the giant bonfire was lit. The guy burst into flames and a dozen children who stood near Jeff began waving their sparklers in delight. After a few minutes had passed, the flayed guy dropped down into the belly of the blaze to an uproar of applause, followed by the first few rockets being shot into the air. Jeff smiled at Ethyl and remarked, "they don't half put on a good show here", as the sky all around them exploded, then dissolved into breathtaking, rainbow-coloured sparks.

XXV

Owen MacRae angrily paced the floor of the living room, his fingers twitching with rage. "I don't know what the fuck she's playing at but I can't keep covering all this shit up."

"They broke their promise," intoned Jenny solemnly, sucking hard on her cigarette.

"I know what they did but Jesus Christ, there's only so much of a blind eye I can get away with turning. This town's so riddled with bodies. It's like fuckin' woodworm or something."

"We can't afford to let anyone break a pact with the Coven. You should know that by now."

"Look, the six kids are easy enough to hide. The parents aren't going to report them so no one else cares. But now, I don't know. We've got three adult stiffs and I know your brothers are getting wise to the fact that something's not right. If we're not careful, they're gonna get in police from the city."

"They can't find anything out or prove anything. Stop being so bloody weak. We're nearly there. Tomorrow there'll be a new Keeper and those two idiots won't even exist."

"I'm not being weak, Jen. I just think we're getting too careless, leaving too much evidence behind."

"It's your task to ensure there is none. Are you trying to tell me you're failing at what we've asked you to do? Is that it?"

"No. Just that… you're moving the goalposts here. There are a shitload more stiffs than you said there'd be."

"Stiffs? Is this all it's about to you? Flesh? Mortal flesh? You're pathetic."

"No, it isn't all this is about but…"

"But what?" Her eyes flashed fire, momentarily. "The six

virgins were culled in the name of far greater laws than you could ever hope to invent or enforce. There are more severe forces at work here than you could possibly imagine."

"Hey, I've seen some shit, I know what you guys do."

"You've seen nothing."

Owen shrugged. "Whatever."

"Do you want out? Is that what you're saying?"

"No…" He shook his head, resignedly. "But…"

"There are no 'buts', Owen," Jenny snarled, flicking her cigarette into a mug half-full of tea dregs and ash. "You made a blood promise."

Owen ran a finger through his spiky black hair. "I know. But the rules have changed. You're killing people left, right and centre!"

"The rules haven't changed. You have. You made a vow to do whatever it took to ensure the new Keeper made a safe passage into the world. You already know the sacrifice I'm making. How the fuck can you stand in front of me and say you've got reservations when you know what I have to do tomorrow?"

Owen shrugged, as Jenny lit up a new cigarette. There was a lengthy period of silence as they stared into each other's eyes.

"Do what you gotta, Jen. I'm going to bed."

"Can I rely on you tomorrow?"

"I don't know what you're talking about," he murmured, throwing his hands into the air and storming upstairs.

Jenny lit another cigarette and began smoking it with shaking hands. Walking towards the mahogany desk, Jenny reached inside the top drawer and pulled out the plain black envelope. She took the tulip petal from within and rubbed it along her lips, kissing it gently and fingering the silver serpent symbol on the paper.

XXVI

Peter was feeling the calming influence of the first joint begin to hit him. Sarah had been kind enough to get a can of Young's Tartan Special Bitter out of the fridge and a pint glass of vodka and orange for herself, pilfered from her father's abundant liquor cabinet.

"Heh," snorted Peter. "This is pretty funny. Raiding your parents' liquor c-cabinet and all."

"Why? You used to do this when you were my age?"

"Nah, but Jeff did. I remember he'd have his mates 'round sometimes when Mum was out. They'd drink about a bottle of vodk-kka and a bottle of gin between the five of 'em and then refill the bottles with water. I remember when Mum found out, she was furious. She'd had a dinner party and invited people round. She was serving gin and tonics, which of c-course was just water and tonic. Her guests didn't want to say anything but eventually one of them piped up and everyone c-c-caught on to what had happened. She virtually pulled him out of his bedroom by his ear!"

Sarah laughed. "So what were you doing when all this was going on?"

"I dunno, I guess I was in my room reading or something. I wasn't really into the whole going out and getting drunk-k thing. That was more Jeff's bag."

"Aw, the studious type."

"No, not really. I was mostly reading pulp or magazines or just any old rubbish. I was very much into escapism."

"Escape from what?"

"I dunno. Mundanity?"

"How could your life be mundane? You grew up in London!" Sarah scoffed, as she handed Peter a newly rolled second joint to spark up.

"I dunno," he replied, taking a long drag. "I guess my growing up experience wasn't quite li-k-ke Jeff's. It was hard to fit in with the stutter and the limp and what-have-you. I didn't have a lot of friends."

"That's so fucking funny. You're like, Peter Davies. In Broadoak, people whisper your name like you're some kind of monster. I imagined you growing up in London as, like, a biker or something. Like, I dunno, the leader of the pack or some shite."

Peter laughed. "No, just some gawky old cripple."

"Oh, stoppit."

"Weirdly enough, Jeff was always the wild child."

"Jeff? But he's a right boring old shite now."

"I dunno. Jeff's pretty much lived life as it's supposed to be done. He went off the rails when he was about fourteen, used to get shitfaced with his mates, go out to c-c-clubs all the time. He used to stay out, spend the night with older women he'd pick-k up. He always loo-kked a bit older than he was. But I guess he got it all out of his system."

"All what?"

"All the sex-x, the drink-king, the fighting. When Mum died, he was eighteen. He dropped out of uni and got a job as an apprentice at this telecoms place in Balham. It was weird, he suddenly got really focused, responsibility hit him hard. At that point, I'd all but given up. I did a few temping jobs, I was just going through the motions. I feel like those years are just gone, lost. I just k-k-kinda drifted. He k-k-kept getting promoted. He worked really fuck-king hard. Oh God, I'm rambling, take this."

He handed Sarah the joint and she took a long drag. He began to giggle. "It's weird the way you look-k back-k on things. I wish I'd done it all different. I wish I'd gone wild like Jeff did. You c-can't do it when you get to my age. You just look ridiculous in a c-club, trying to act c-c-cool." Peter grinned, self-deprecatingly. "God, I sound like a ccliché."

"You don't. You just remind me how much I wanna get out of Broadoak. Jesus, at least you have clubs in London to go to. There's nothing 'round here. There's a few places in Gloucester but trying to get the bus back after ten o'clock's impossible."

"Yeah? Buses run all night in London."

"I know. So what are the London clubs like?"

"Uh. Loud. I dunno. I don't tend to go to very many. I went to a few when I was about twenty two, twenty three, but never really got into it. I think-k people go there to pick-k up and I was never any good at that."

"How come?"

"I dunno. It all felt like bullshit. I gave up c-caring, really. Lik-ke I did about most things." He snorted.

There was a short interlude as Sarah took a drag of her joint and passed it to Peter. He drained the remainder of his beer and began to smoke.

"You want another? My dad has loads."

"Sure, thanks."

Sarah went to fetch Peter another can from the fridge. He watched through the kitchen door as she bent over to pick it up and felt an all-too-familiar stirring in his lap. He fought against it and tried thinking about the least erotic things he could conceive of – old Mrs Deering in her underwear, his father lying handless beneath the ground, the caustic smell of his old prison cell – but it was more difficult than usual to hold back. Ordinarily, he would get aroused looking at girls who could never be anything more than fantasies. They were no more interested in him than they would be a barium lunch. But here was Sarah Hobson, as young and beautiful as any of them, virtually offering herself to him on a plate. He tried to hide his erection by pulling his shirt down and felt self-consciously inexperienced all of a sudden. He took another long drag on the joint, in an effort to subdue his nerves. It was strange how there were a few things that didn't get easier with age. That he wasn't able to get rid of by ceasing to care. These urges ran deep in him – beyond his rational thought, an animal lust. *Tell it to the judge,* his mind chided, remembering that any sexual contact with Sarah would be deemed statutory rape in a court of law.

"So when did you lose your virginity?" asked Sarah, smiling and tossing him the can of beer. He caught it and immediately returned one hand to his crotch, hoping she hadn't already noticed the protrusion beneath his trousers.

"Sarah!" he scalded. Still desperately trying to fight his instincts, he feigned shock.

"No really, come on. I wanna hear. Don't be so shy."

"I'm not being shy. I just... I dunno. I feel a bit uncomfortable talking about it."

"Have more beer then!" She hooted with laughter. She even began pouring herself another strong, large glass of vodka and orange.

He took her advice and took a hefty swig of the Tartan Special and another drag of the joint.

"I don't need to hear the whole story," she said, coyly. "I just want to know how old you were. I'm curious."

"It was... quite late."

"What? Like eighteen? Twenty?"

Peter shifted uncomfortably as Sarah sat back down next to him on the couch, splashing a little of her drink on the cushion. "I dunno."

"Oh come on, of course you do. Tell me."

"It's a bit... embarrassing. I don't usually tell people this k-kind of thing. Of c-c-c-course, people don't usually ask." He shrugged and took another swig of beer as Sarah stole the joint from out of his hand, playfully.

"You're still a virgin, aren't you?" she said, grinning widely.

"Actually…" he paused. "Yeah."

"Oh my God, that's so fucking funny!" She burst into laughter.

"Oh thanks!" he grumbled, sarcastically.

"No, stupid, not that. Just… well. A virgin sex offender. It's pretty ironic, don't you think?"

Even Peter laughed out loud, followed by a string of giggles he couldn't hold back. "Yeah, I guess, when you put it that way. But you know I never… I only…" He paused and blinked. "Why the Hell am I telling you this? Forget it." He was feeling the effect of the drugs now.

"I know what you did. I've read about it in the papers," she said.

Peter's face turned serious. "Then why the Hell are you sat here talk-k-king to me?"

"I dunno. I actually like you, weirdo pervert sex beast or whatever."

Peter laughed again.

"Seriously. You actually have stuff to say, stories to tell, opinions on things. Have you any idea how boring everyone is 'round here?"

"Err, well, I've k-k-kind of gleaned it over the past few days."

"The kids at school are the worst."

"What?" Peter laughed. "You mean you don't have a boyfriend?"

"God no."

"No one you're even a teensy bit interested in?" He was teasing her now.

"No! They're all wankers. There's this one boy who follows me around everywhere. He's just so annoying though. He's got, like, no interest in anything."

"Oh? Who's he then?"

"His name's Johnny Piper."

"Ah, the newsagent's lad?"

"Yeah. He's so fucking irritating. He just won't leave me alone."

"I heard he had the flu at the moment."

"Really?" Sarah thought for a second. "I guess that would explain where he's been the last couple of days. Oh well, I don't miss him."

Both took large gulps of their drink and Sarah began rolling up a third joint. Peter was feeling unusually relaxed and didn't even care that the conversation had gone further than he ordinarily would have been comfortable with. He felt amused and entertained by Sarah's company and younger than he had done in years, if not ever. Peter realised, as Sarah completed rolling the joint, that the pair of them had lapsed into silence. He wished for some background noise or some music.

"Oh!" he exclaimed suddenly, making both of them jump a little. "You said you were going to play me some of that music you lik-k-ke."

"Oh yeah! You'll have to come upstairs though. We don't have a stereo down here."

Peter woozily stood up and felt a little disorientated. The room was tilting slightly and he had to blink repeatedly in order to set it straight. He followed Sarah as she climbed the stairs carefully, visibly a bit drunk and trying not to slip. She opened the door to her bedroom and turned the light on, revealing the wall of posters. Peter had to laugh.

"What?" she asked, alarmed by his reaction.

"Nice wallpaper!"

"Oh, the posters. Well, yeah. I like to have them up, y'know? Reminds me that I'm a real person with things I actually care about."

There wasn't much Peter could say to that. They both stepped into the room and Peter surveyed it. It was a large room, not insufferably messy although not tidy either. A few random clothes were scattered on the floor but the bed was made and the posters lent it a strange vibrancy. Peter's eyes strayed to the giant swastika flag atop the bed.

"Err…" he said, pointing to it with bemused disapproval.

"Oh," Sarah blushed a little. "I bought that a while back. I liked the colours more than anything. I'm not, like, a nazi or anything. You know this guy?" She changed the subject and pointed to a large poster of Alice Cooper, a black haired, dishevelled-looking rock star dressed head to toe in black leather, with black eye make-up and a scowl. "Alice fuckin' Cooper."

"Yeah, I know him. I think-k Jeff saw him live years ago."

"No way? Jeff saw Alice live? Wow. That's so cool. He played a gig at the Gloucester Guild Hall a few months back but Dad wouldn't let me go."

"I can't say I'm really familiar with his stuff."

"Oh, you have to hear this."

Sarah fumbled around in a messy looking pile of cassettes stacked up next to a large stereo system on the wooden dresser. She pulled one out of its case and slid it into the player. Peter noticed the name of the album was "Love it to Death".

"I always skip track one," she whispered, pushing a button and all of a sudden the room came alive with an almighty pounding of drums. Peter's addled mind sucked up the music and it seemed to reverberate in his skull. A snaking, complicated bassline wrapped itself around his senses and caressed his ears. A wailing guitar kicked in and made Peter flush a little. He closed his eyes and began to drift into the song, as a gravely voice full of pain and passion began to sing:

"Lines form on my face and hands… Lines form from my ups and downs…"

When he opened them again, he saw Sarah had begun

to dance in front of the stereo, oscillating her hips in time with the music.

"I'm in the middle, without any plans... I'm a boy and I'm a man..."

Peter nodded his head up and down in time with the music but didn't feel he had the energy to join her in the dance. She leant over him, still moving her waist and shoulders and offered him the rest of the lit joint in her hand. He took it and enjoyed a long drag, as Sarah floated back to the stereo and began singing along with the music.

"I gotta get away! I gotta get out of this place, go runnin' in outer space! Yeah yeah!"

Peter had never really been a huge music lover but at that moment, its appeal suddenly made sense. Even the air felt as if it were pulsating with the lush rhythms emitting from the speakers. Sarah's voice, as she sang along, was entirely unself-conscious, she believed in every word. Peter began listening to the lyrics and had a realisation they were talking about him.

"Got a baby's brain and old man's heart... took eighteen years just to get this far..."

"This is fuck-king incredible," he said, in a daze.

"Don't even know what I'm talkin' about... I'm in the middle, the middle of doubt..."

"I told you," Sarah grinned.

He took a final swig from his beer and crushed the can, watching Sarah dancing and growing progressively aroused. She swished her long, black hair side to side wildly, as the song built to a furious crescendo. Time seemed neither too fast nor too slow. It just lost all sense of proportion, as the sounds seemed to swirl around Peter's head like transparent sonic eels.

"I like it, love it, like it, love it!" she howled breathlessly in time with the music, gyrating herself into a frenzy.

As the music stopped abruptly, the surreal mood seemed

to break as Sarah tripped and fell noisily to the floor. Peter snapped out of his trance and began to laugh hysterically.

"Don't laugh, you shite. I've hurt my bloody knee!"

She rolled up her trouser leg, revealing a small red graze bleeding a little, dripping red onto her unblemished alabaster flesh. Peter grinned at her. "You'd best put a plaster on that."

"Yeah. I'll be right back, ok? You just sit and listen to this."

Sarah left the room and Peter readjusted his ears to the music. A new song was playing now, all crazy, jitterbug drumming and staccato bass with Alice Cooper's voice crooning sarcastically over the top, *"we've still got a long way to go"*. Peter laughed to himself. It was unbelievable how much the lyrics seemed to coincide with the situation. He knew Sarah was trying to seduce him, albeit a little clumsily. Both of them were so inexperienced, it was almost comical. *"We've still got a long way to go"* indeed. Maybe it was the drugs? Maybe it was pure chance? Or maybe some grand cosmic plan beyond his comprehension? He felt suddenly like a tiny puppet under the gaze and control of a great-unseen force that he would never be able to defeat or understand.

He lay back on the bed, staring up at the posters. He closed his eyes and again became lost in the music. As the track ended, he heard a click and the sound of the door moving. He opened them slowly and found the light had been switched off. Sarah stood above him, naked except for a pair of black lace panties and a small plaster on her knee. A new song was beginning. Slow tribal drumming, a short loop of pounding bass and tom, repeating hypnotically. Peter tried to speak but realised he had lost the ability. Sarah put her finger to her lips and her wide brown eyes spoke to him, telling him she understood and that there was suddenly no need for words.

As a grinding roar of guitar burst into the track, Sarah leant over Peter, pushing her small pubescent breasts near his face. She looked beautiful in the strange glow that was lighting the room. Fireworks from the nearby park still kept the sky ablaze with colour and this brightness burnt through the windowpane, reflected down from the deep red of the swastika flag, bathing the entire room with a wash of crimson.

Alice Cooper on the stereo let out a chilling scream, a feral roar of such animalistic rage and lust, it sent vibrations through Peter's body. He could control himself no longer and pulled Sarah close to him, kissing her tender flesh all over with unbridled fervour, obsessively breathing her in, savouring the smell of her skin, the strangely sweet taste of her, mixed with the beer and smoke. She returned his eagerness with equally unrestrained excitement, tearing off his shirt and rubbing her face into his chest, nibbling his flesh and running her hands along him.

Soon both of them were naked and writhing crazily atop the bedsheets. They could have been everywhere and nowhere all at once, but not Broadoak. The inanity of the day was washed clean away by their furious lust and the lunatic rhythms of the Alice Cooper Band, as they made love beneath the eerie glow of the skeletal swastika and the flare of fireworks. It was otherworldly and yet entirely natural. Beyond their control.

Alice Cooper's voice rang free and true through the speakers, spitting out lyrics, the cry of a man on the edge of madness: *"Bodies! Clutching and biting, my soul's caught on fire! My evil is now and I'm caught up in desire! Everything I'm living for is all that I am, liking it and loving it that's all in the plan."*

The lovers became locked together as music rose to fever pitch. What seemed like eternity passed between them until finally the drums erupted into a cacophonous climax. The sheer force of the sound engulfed the room. Alice whispered:

"Black juju."

Then everything became silent.

XXVII

Jeff stood by the side of his father's grave, surprised to see it was still open. Some token piles of soil lay atop the coffin but, for some reason, Selwyn had not completed the work. The golden cross and the wreath were missing from the box.

"Thieving little pikeys," muttered Jeff under his breath. He wasn't a religious man by any stretch, so not bothered whether his father would be buried with a cross or not. He was just mildly disgusted by how the local kids would steal anything, even from a dead man.

He stood and stared into the grave for a while, musing on the Davies bloodline. He had always thought it would be continued but now it seemed like the name would die with him and his siblings. At thirty-five, Jeff had resigned himself to the fact that it was too late to start a family. With Peter's troubles, there was no chance of his having children. The hysterectomy had ensured Jenny wouldn't either.

As for Jeff, he'd had his chance years ago and blown it. He'd met Natasha during his brief stint at university. They had stuck together for six years but eventually their differences and the time consumed by Jeff's job had destroyed them. He never had the energy to try to make things work and all the plans they'd made in the heady early days of the relationship crumbled like a house of cards beneath the weight of adulthood and responsibility. He idly wondered what had happened to her but knew full well that her ambition for a husband and children would have got her what she wanted by now. It was unlikely she ever thought of him at all.

He felt suddenly so lonely, as if a surge of ice had shot up his veins. He looked around the empty graveyard and wanted to cry. The night sky had calmed down from earlier on, the fireworks long since having died out. It was now black apart from the moonlight's struggling to be seen beneath ominous grey clouds that crawled through the darkness. The mist from the nearby forest was rising. Jeff found that he couldn't see from the gravesite back to the church – a relatively short distance – through the blanket of fog that was forming. He hoped that Selwyn would hurry up. After the excitement of the bonfire, the miserable silence of midnight now seemed so oppressive that Jeff half-wanted to throw himself in his father's grave and wait for the soil to smother him.

"Hello boyo," a voice emerged from behind him. As Jeff squinted to see through the fog, he made out the tall, skinny figure of Selwyn walking towards him, shovel in hand. Stood in the murk of the deserted cemetery with a complete stranger, he suddenly felt irrationally afraid and wished he had brought some kind of weapon himself.

"What did you want?" Jeff tried to remain as authoritative as he could.

"I thought you should know what's going on in this town. What happened to your father. What's going to happen to you, so it will, if you're not careful."

"My dad drowned."

Selwyn laughed. "Don't play stupid, boyo. You know as well as I do, that's not what happened."

"Is it to do with Dad's hands?"

"Amongst other things."

"Alright," Jeff was growing cold and impatient. Although his padded Barbour jacket kept him warm normally, the air in the cemetery was unnaturally freezing. "Just cut to it. Dad was murdered, right?"

"Aye, murdered so he was, boyo."

"By whom?"

"The Coven. The Keepers of the Devil's Garden."

Jeff closed his eyes and took a deep breath. Selwyn was

obviously some kind of madman. "Riiiight…" he said, slowly and sarcastically. "And they would be?"

"I knew you wouldn't believe me, but I can prove it. The Coven runs this town, boyo. You're either with them, to some extent or another, or you disappear. They have power. Serious power. They practice black magic, the worst kind of necromancy."

"Necromancy? Look, I'm sorry, it would freeze the balls off a brass monkey out here. I appreciate you trying to help and ordinarily I'd love to build a campfire, knock back a beer and swap spook stories with you but I'm not going to catch pneumonia just to listen to you babble on about bloody necromancy. Not tonight, thanks."

"Open the coffin." Selwyn's voice was suddenly confident. He was grinning in the gloom, gripping his shovel tightly.

"What? You want me to go down there so you can hit me with the bloody shovel? Piss off! You're nuts!" Jeff was about to stalk off, when Selwyn thrust the shovel out and forced it into his hands.

"Fine!" the Welshman snarled. "I'll go down there, but so help me God, you'd better be ready with this shovel to hit what comes out of that box."

Jeff needed no further proof to ascertain the other man was quite insane, but felt better for at least now being the one with a weapon. He nodded and tried to keep a straight face as Selwyn hopped into the grave and began wrestling with the coffin lid.

"Ok," he shouted to Jeff. "Move in closer now. I'm going to lift the lid, so I am. You have to strike fast and watch you don't knock my block off."

Jeff moved towards the grave and watched as Selwyn pulled up the box lid. There was a deafening shriek of unearthly high pitch, as a figure shot upwards from within. Jeff stared in abject horror as he saw the eyeless face of his father's corpse, flesh peeling from its face, maggots crawling in the hollow, pallid cheeks. The skin around the lips was crumbling, exposing vile teeth that clamped down on a mouthful of worms. The corpse was trying frantically to scramble out of the box, waving its handless arms impotently in the air.

"For God's sake, boyo, hit the fucking thing!" screamed Selwyn, hiding behind the coffin lid.

Jeff snapped out of his terrified paralysis and swung the shovel for all he was worth at the unearthly beast, striking a blow to its head and knocking it back into the coffin.

"Oh, just give me that," growled Selwyn, snatching the shovel from Jeff's hands and discarding the large oak lid on the ground. He stood over the corpse and brought the shovel down between its neck and its head, decapitating it, as a ghastly crunching of bone echoed through the air.

"What the fuck was that?" shouted Jeff, his voice wavering and thin.

"They put a protection spell on the coffin. They didn't want anyone getting a look at your father's corpse and living to tell the tale."

"Ok, look, you need to start at the start before giving me all this spell bollocks. What in God's name is going on?" Selwyn's eyes darkened and he spoke slowly. "Oh, trust me boyo, there's nothing going on in His name here in Broadoak. There is just evil here. They are the Keepers of the Devil's Garden. Their symbol is the serpent. The Coven exists to plant seeds of evil in the Earth, to grow corrupted flowers of flesh and blood for the Devil to admire. He wants flesh, he craves sin. We tend his garden with these things."

"We?" Jeff stepped back a little.

Selwyn laughed grimly. "Of course. As I said, you're either with them or you disappear. I'm pretty far down the food chain, as these things go. I just dig graves. I don't even know who the elders actually are."

"The elders?"

"The elders are the ones that perform the blood rites."

Jeff snorted. "Somehow, you know, I just guessed there were going to be blood rites involved. Is this what they killed Dad for?"

"No, your father had had enough, so he had. He's old enough to have seen the rites a few times now. He decided it was wrong and tried to stop it. That's why he tried to save Katie Brown. She was to be the sixth virgin."

"I don't follow."

"Every six years, the elders offer up six virgins to the Devil's Garden. On the sixty-sixth year, there is a new Keeper born."

"What's a Keeper?"

Selwyn took a deep breath and began explaining in the slow, almost patronising tones of a schoolteacher. "The Keeper is the strongest of all the elders. The most powerful magician. The Keeper is fuelled by the purity of the sixty-six virgin sacrifices that have preceded the Coming. Before death, they remove the sources of sin, the sources of pleasure. They slice off the nipples, they cut out the clitoris, chop off the penis."

Jeff winced.

"The energy from this purity is inverted, turned into undiluted evil by the rites that occur every sixty-sixth year. The Keeper has to be a direct descendent of the Devil's own bloodline. It has always been this way. There must be a sacrifice. A spilling of the unholy blood of the old Keeper and any surviving members of their family. Then the new Keeper must be born from the seed of an incestuous union."

"So Dad tried to stop them sacrificing this Katie girl?"

"Yes, God only knows why, the mad fool. But this year is the sixty-sixth year since the birth of the old Keeper. A new one is to be born tomorrow, on the sixth night after Samhain."

Jeff felt confused and sickened. "And they kill children?"

"That's not all they do."

There was an uncomfortable silence.

"Why are you telling me this? Why are you betraying these... people?"

"The whole town has to be in on it, but most of them don't want to give up their children to the Coven. They're fine to be a part of it until the wheel turns round to their kids and then they get scared, they don't want to make that sacrifice." Selwyn began nervously chewing his fingernails. "My Dad was a coward. He didn't want to risk me being one of the sacrifices. I was ten years old. He made sure I wasn't a virgin any more."

Jeff stared at Selwyn in horror, as the younger man rolled his sleeves up.

"He didn't leave any scars on my body. But believe me, I can still feel them." He rubbed his hands around his wrists. "Like right here where he held me down."

Another uncomfortable silence. Jeff held Selwyn's stare for as long as he could before looking away.

"Jesus," muttered Jeff.

"I want them stopped, so I do," the Welshman stated powerfully. "I want Broadoak to be a normal town again."

"What do you expect me to do? I'm just going to call the police, you realise."

"The police 'round here won't do anything, as you well know. Call the Gloucester police if you want, but what are you going to tell them? Someone's playing around with your dad's corpse and a bloke you've never met before told you a scary ghost story?"

"There must be evidence somewhere. Where is this Devil's Garden? Where did they bury all the kids?"

"I'll show you. I'll take you out there tomorrow."

"And then what?"

"We can stop them. Before the new Keeper is born."

"But why us? And how many others are going to help?"

"There's no one else. No one else is going to break the pact with the Coven and I'm not going 'round the town asking about it, neither. I'd get myself killed, if I did. You're from the outside so I reckon I can trust you. Can I?"

"Do you have a plan?"

"I have a hunting rifle," Selwyn grinned.

"I need to talk to my brother, Peter. I'm not doing anything without him."

"That's fine."

"So how are we getting there? To this place?"

"You have a car, don't you?"

"Yeah."

"Ok, so you can drive me and your brother up there tomorrow. It's not far. It's up on Symonds Yat rock."

"That's the big rock that overlooks the Forest of Dean isn't it?"

"Aye, so it is."

"Alright. What time is this… thing happening?"

"It'll happen midday. We could do with leaving Broadoak by nine at the latest."

"Fine. I'll drive my car up to the Bull's Head Inn and meet you there."

"No!" hissed Selwyn. "We can't be seen together. I'll meet you by the sign outside the village. The 'Welcome to Broadoak' one, ok? Nine'o'clock?"

"Sure. I'll see you then."

Jeff began to walk off through the freezing fog and towards the church, fumbling a little and navigating with his arms in front of him. As he put some distance between himself and Selwyn, the Welshman seemed to just vanish into the mist. It was eerie and the suffocating silence all around was unnerving. Jeff felt himself shiver and not entirely from the cold.

He had to tell Peter about this immediately but was

unsure what to even say. As he wove his way slowly down the deserted Conker Lane, he began to feel his heartbeat accelerate. The trees were bowing slightly in the wind and creaking, but aside from that, there was no sound to be heard. He began thinking of the sight of his father's animated corpse leaping out of the coffin. How had the Welshman done it? Was it a conjuring trick? It couldn't be real. None of this could be real. He had to talk to Peter. He had to find out what was happening.

As he looked up at the pale moon, its faint spectral glow battling to be seen behind the blanket of mist, all he could see forming in the air before him were the dead, hollow eyes of his father, watching him. He screamed into the night and began scrambling down the lane back to the town. He wished he were safely asleep in a warm bed, somewhere nice in London, totally at peace alongside his old flame Natasha. The night was vicious and very much alive here in Broadoak.

XXVIII

Owen MacRae lay on Jennifer Davies's bed, his arms folded behind his head, his eyes gazing out of the window and at the moon cloaked in mist. He was feeling utterly dejected and, for the first time in the fifteen years since he joined the Coven, wondering what on Earth he was doing and why. He had joined because of the power. Even though he would never have the supernatural abilities of those who were in the Keeper's bloodline, the Coven itself as an entity was what kept Broadoak living in fear. He wanted to be on the right side of that.

For years he had helped in fairly minor ways to cover up what was happening in Broadoak, but with the Coming of the New Keeper approaching, he had been elevated up through the ranks and was suddenly part of the inner circle. He had single-handedly buried the six sexless, mutilated children up on Symonds Yat rock this year, his shaking hands lowering their small, cold bones into the black soil of the earth and muttering the unholy incantations in the language of the angels, as Jenny had taught him to do. But he knew he wasn't ready for this.

He just wanted power as an outlet for the otherwise impotent rage that ran through his veins like hot lava. He might like pushing people around a bit, but he didn't want to bury children. Each night as he closed his eyes, he was still haunted by the red, congealed holes between their legs, their empty eyes, imploring him not to put them in the ground, as if they knew what unearthly, horrible fate awaited them after death. He clenched his teeth and wished he knew how to get away from all of this. Maybe he would just run. Get away from Broadoak, flee up North somewhere. The police in Gloucester were already sniffing around Broadoak. They suspected something, he was sure. There were too many loose ends to tie up – the Hobson girl, those bloody London brothers. They were all out there tonight in Broadoak, any one of them could uncover the whole thing and blow it out into the open. What then? Prison? Death? Owen closed his eyes tightly and waited for the images of the dead children to dissipate.

He heard a click as the door moved.

"Owen." It was Jenny's voice.

"What?" he mumbled, reluctantly opening his eyes.

She was stood in the doorway, wearing a translucent silk kimono. "I'm sorry. I know all this is hard on you."

He shifted position as she walked sultrily into the room, her blond hair glowing almost silver in the ghostly light from outside. "I dunno, I think I'm in too deep. There's too much I can't hide now. I'm scared, Jen."

"Don't be." She approached him and put a finger to his lips. "There's nothing to be afraid of."

"But the Hobson girl or your brothers. I know they'll be onto us. They all know something's not right. What do we do if they get in the police from Gloucester?" She was almost purring her words now, stroking his forehead softly. "They won't. You won't have to worry about them after tomorrow anyway. Can I still rely on you? You will be at the ceremony, yes?"

"I don't have much choice, do I?"

She answered his question in the form of a kiss, a long, lingering one that took Owen's breath away and aroused his passions, in spite of his earlier anxiety. "Better?" she asked, with a giggle as she undid the silk belt and opened up the kimono, whilst straddling his waist.

"Oh yeah," he replied with a half-grin that exposed his firebrand teeth. Whether or not he was going to run before daybreak, the least he could do was to stick around and get some of this, he thought to himself.

She took off his trousers slowly and ran her mouth down his legs, kissing and gently biting his skin. He moaned with pleasure and closed his eyes, feeling her move back up and position herself on top of him, sliding his now swollen cock into her soft, wet hollow. She began rocking back and forth, slowly, kissing him, biting his neck and holding his wrists down lightly.

"Let me touch you, baby," he slurred. She smiled cheekily and shook her head, applying a little more force to his wrists, erotically pinning him to the bed.

She began to flick her tongue around his nipples and he let out another, almost imperceptible gasp. Her cunt tightened around him and all at once he felt himself on the verge of climax. She kept pushing her hips into him and he couldn't hold back. As he literally screamed, feeling the hot rush of ecstasy shooting through his cock, she moved her mouth from one nipple to the next, rapidly. The pleasure that shook his body had overrode his senses and it was only when he looked down and saw the blood that he could suddenly feel the tremendous sting of pain.

She had bitten both of his nipples off. She raised her head and smiled at him, a trickle of crimson dew dribbling down her chin.

"What the fuck!?" he shouted and frantically tried to free himself. Jenny's grip on his wrists had tightened and when he tried to force his lower body upwards, he found he was unable to. Her cunt was acting as a vacuum trapping him inside her, and her hips imprisoned him on the bed.

He looked at her face and saw her eyes begin to roll upwards. As they rolled completely back into her head, the two white orbs were suddenly replaced by pinkish flesh – his nipples! She stared down at him through the nipple-eyes and laughed wildly.

"All we were asking you to do, Owen, was turn a blind eye!" she howled in ghastly singsong.

"Jesus, dear God, what is this? Oh my God!" he began babbling and yelling, still desperately struggling to break free.

He felt an incredible tearing pain in his groin as she lowered herself and tightened even more around him, this time engulfing his entire crotch. There was a hideous ripping sound, almost like wet Velcro and the lower half of the bed began to turn crimson. He looked down at her body and saw two small spheres of lumpy flesh moving upwards across her midriff.

"My balls! My fucking balls!"

The two lumps crept up towards her breasts and became oversized, almost comical protrusions on the end of her nipples, like giant cherries.

"Suck them," she ordered, solemn-faced, no longer laughing, those disgusting nipple-eyes weeping blood down her face. She lowered her breasts to Owen's face and forced one into his mouth. He tried to bite it, snapping his teeth frantically, trying not to black out from the pain and blood loss from his crotch. Finally he pierced through her flesh and pulled his head back hard, detaching the vile appendage that protruded from her nipple. She laughed and pushed his head back onto the bed. He vomited hard as he felt the shape of his own testicle rolling onto his tongue and heading for his throat. She forced his mouth closed and he felt himself begin to choke on his vomit and the horrible fleshy sphere that was now blocking his airway.

The last noise Owen MacRae made was a pathetic, whimpering retching sound as his eyes rolled back in his head and he lost consciousness. Jenny Davies held open her eyelids, as one might to remove a contact lens, and the two bloodied, severed nipples fell out onto Owen's face. Her real eyes now glowed yellow in the darkness of the room. She began grinding her hips again on the still stiff cock of his corpse and rocked herself to overwhelming climax.

***

Across the town, in another moonlit bedroom, the voice of Alice Cooper still sung softly from a stereo that had been turned down to an almost inaudible volume.

"See my lonely life unfold, I see it every day…"

Sarah Hobson lay awake in the darkness, silently mouthing along with the tape. She was scared. She looked down at Peter Davies, lying beside her in the single bed, snoring softly and became terrified. She knew he was due to leave for London tomorrow, but also that she couldn't bear for him to. The night had been an incredible one. She had finally found a companion, one that made her feel not just alive, but alive in someone else's skin, someone else's mind. She didn't feel like boring Sarah Hobson from boring old Broadoak any more. She felt special with Peter, wanted even, and she didn't even have to do anything except be herself.

But right now, in the creepy glow of the moon, in the lonely darkness of the silent small hours before the dawn, it felt so fleeting, so uncertain. It had all happened so fast and without words. What was going through his mind as he lay there now? Sarah had never lain here with anyone else before. She wasn't used to this awful feeling that they could be gone by sunrise.

"Sun arise, come every morning," sang Alice quietly on the stereo, as if reading her thoughts. *"Sun arise, come every morning, bringing back the warmth to the ground."*

PART THREE: SPITE AND MALICE

The Sweet Kiss of Filth
A Flea Turns To Gold

"Cursing their lovers, cursing the Bible. Hallowed be my name." – Alice Cooper

XXIX

Jeff slept uneasily on the living room sofa at Jenny's house. It had been nearly two in the morning by the time he had arrived there and he was too scared and angry to sleep. He had been to the Bull's Head Inn immediately after his midnight meeting with Selwyn and had tossed a couple of pebbles up at Peter's window. There had been no response. He had knocked on the front door and the landlord had answered. There were still a few heavy-jacketed, bearded farmers sat in the bar area – a lock-in. The landlord had informed Jeff that Peter had not actually returned to his room that night and, after a brief scour of the streets before deciding he was freezing half to death, Jeff had retreated back to Jenny's.

Peter's disappearance from the Bull's Head had got him worried and every time he closed his eyes now he saw macabre images of his brother, handless and eyeless, springing from the dirty soil of an unmarked grave. After one too many times of waking up from half-sleeps, gasping and sweating, Jeff turned on the light and went into the kitchen to make a mug of coffee. The clock on the wall informed him it was half past six in the morning already. He took his coffee into the living room and switched on the TV at a low volume.

He sat, sipping on his drink and vegetating in front of the perfectly plastic Breakfast TV presenters. They babbled inanely to a bleary-eyed pop singer, who clearly wasn't used to being awake so early. Jeff contemplated Peter's whereabouts in a slightly calmer frame of mind than previously. The night had made him jittery and he was glad the dawn was now approaching. At least whatever was happening in Broadoak would finally be resolved today and he could get back to London, hopefully.

As he recounted the events of the previous day to himself in his mind, a fact so incredibly obvious that he nearly smacked himself in the face for having forgotten it before suddenly sprang to mind. Peter had been spending the evening with Sarah Hobson. It put him off finishing the rest of his coffee to think about it but... *what if Peter had spent the night at the Hobson house?*

Jeff put on a thick Barbour jacket and some gloves, heading outside to his car. The windscreen was frosted over and he spent a frustrating ten minutes scraping it down with his credit card. He turned the car heater on for a further ten minutes until it was finally warm enough to sit down in. As he always took the train to work in London, he'd forgotten just how irritating driving first thing in the morning was throughout the winter months.

He drove across town to the Hobson house and was a little unsure of how to proceed. Did he just ring the doorbell and hope that Sarah answered? What if her parents answered? What could he say? *"Oh, excuse me, I was just wondering if my thirty-three year-old brother had stayed the night here with your fourteen year-old daughter?"* – somehow that didn't seem to wash. He thought once more of his father's corpse in the graveyard and of his desperation for Peter to join him in whatever this Selwyn character was planning. He took a deep breath and rang the doorbell, crossing his fingers behind his back and hoping for the best.

A few minutes passed. Jeff watched his breath form little clouds of vapour in front of him. Eventually the front door to the Hobson' house opened and a tired-looking Sarah answered it. She brushed a web of tangled hair from her face and looked confusedly at Jeff.

"Huh?" was all she could manage to ask.

"Hi Sarah," Jeff began, starting to nervously scratch his

ears and nose. "Err, you were with my brother last night, yeah?"

"Yeah, I saw Peter last night."

"You don't happen to know where he is now do you? I really urgently need to talk to him."

Sarah glanced out of the door behind Jeff and saw the car, its engine still running, pumping hot exhaust fumes out into the wintry air. "I'm sorry, I haven't seen him," she said, as icily as the weather outside.

"Sarah," Jeff pleaded. "I'm serious, if you know where he is…"

She was about to close the door when all of a sudden, Peter himself appeared behind her. "It's alright, Sarah," he said, putting his hand on her shoulder. "Jeff, what is it?"

"I need to talk to you."

There was uncomfortable silence. Peter lifted an eyebrow.

"Alone," Jeff added, at last.

Sarah looked at Peter who smiled benignly at her. "Would you mind?" he asked, softly. "Just for a minute or two. I'll be right back."

"Whatever." Sarah rolled her eyes and walked up the stairs, leaving the two brothers stood in the living room.

"Look-k-k, Jeff, it's not what you think it is," Peter said, glancing awkwardly at the floor.

"Peter," Jeff began, in an exasperated tone. "I honestly don't care. That's not why I'm here. It's your life, mate, and if you want to fuck it up, that's none of my business any more."

"I'm not fuck-k-k…"

"Peter, honestly, save it." Jeff raised a hand. "I need to talk to you about something else. I want you to come with me today."

"Bac-k-k to London?"

"No, I'm going up Symonds Yat rock. This is going to

sound crazy but you were right, there is something wrong with this place. There's... God, this sounds ridiculous. I don't even know how to put it. This guy, this gravedigger, was telling me about a group of people in Broadoak who... who kill children. They tried to kill Katie Brown, the girl who was in the papers, who was supposed to be with Dad when he died, remember?"

"I remember."

"Well, apparently Dad was trying to save her from them when he went missing. Apparently, they... they killed Dad."

"What makes you believe this guy?"

"I don't know. I don't even know as I do. He showed me something that was... very strange. I can't really explain. He's taking me out to the rock today. He's got a plan for how to stop these people but he needs help."

"Why doesn't he just go to the police?"

"He reckons MacRae's in on it all and the city police won't give a shit because there's no tangible evidence he can show them, or something. I don't know. That's why I'm going today. I want to find out more. But I want you with me. If this is something to do with Dad then it seems only fair. Are you in?"

Peter laughed. "This is so fuck-ked up. The other day, it was me telling you that something was wrong in Broadoak-k and you were all 'oh no, there's nothing wrong'. Now you're here trying to get me to go c-c-climbing up bloody Symonds Yat with some loony gravedigger because you think – and let me get this straight – that the people of Broadoak-k are k-killing children?"

"What can I say?"

"The other day, when we bro-k-ke into the funeral home, it was me who had nothing to lose. Now I feel maybe I do."

Jeff smiled weakly. "Look, the worst that can happen is that it'll be a waste of time and this Selwyn bloke's talking out of his arse."

"Selwyn? Selwyn Jarvis?" Sarah's voice appeared from the top of the stairs. She began walking down. "You're joking?"

"What?" said Jeff defensively, shocked that she had been eavesdropping.

"Ugh. He's such a creepy little shite."

Jeff snorted. "Yeah, he is. I'll give you that."

"I think you're right about something weird going on though," she continued, uninvited. "My parents didn't come home last night. I just checked their rooms and neither of them are here."

"When did you last see them?" asked Peter, concerned.

"I dunno. I saw Dad briefly yesterday morning." Sarah paused to think. "Last time I saw them both was in the kitchen. Some woman had come to see Dad about the shop and he was all upset about it. He had a letter or something. Oh there it is."

Sarah's eyes moved towards the coffee table by the side of the couch. There was a plain black envelope on top of it. Jeff went to pick it up and opened it, revealing a piece of paper with two entwined silver serpents on it. A tulip petal dropped out and landed on the floor.

"Oh my God," Jeff exclaimed. "Jenny has one just like this at home."

Peter was staring at the pile of mail stacked up by the front door. There was another black envelope down there. "Look-k," he said, opening it to reveal identical contents to the first.

"What the fuck?" asked Sarah.

"The serpents..." Peter mumbled. "Just like on Dad's ring."

Sarah stretched her fingers and they all looked at the serpent design on Guy Davies' old ring.

"Well, there's your proof," remarked Jeff, bluntly.

"There's definitely something going on. The Hobsons have gone missing and the silver serpent design… God, I'd forgot all about Dad's ring and the letter when he said it but…" Jeff trailed off.

"What? When who said what?" Peter urged.

"Selwyn. When he said the serpent was the emblem of the Coven."

"Coven?" Sarah spat, derisively.

"Oh, look, I can't explain. Peter, just come with me. Selwyn'll tell you everything on the way, ok? I said I was meeting him soon."

"Fine."

Sarah looked suddenly upset.

"Just give me two sec-c-conds, ok-k?"

Jeff nodded and walked out of the front door, shaking his head. "Meet you at the car."

When they were alone, Peter grabbed Sarah by the arms and looked her square in the eyes. "I promise, I will be back-k. Whatever happens."

"You're not going back to London?"

"I don't know. I don't know what I'm doing. Let me sort Jeff out first. But whatever, I'll be bac-k-k here tonight. To see you."

"I don't want you to go," she averted her eyes from his as she said this.

"Sarah, I don't want to go now. I really don't. You have to believe me. As soon as I'm finished with all this crap, I will be here. With you."

He kissed her, intensely, almost pushing his face into hers. She returned the kiss with matching ardour. They both looked at each other as if something else should be said at this point but neither quite knew what or how to say it.

"Later," she said, smiling resignedly, as he threw on his leather jacket and bolted out the door after Jeff, his limp barely distinguishable when he moved at such speed.

XXX

The ancient crone stood atop the rock, looking down at the mighty river that ran below. She took a deep breath of the air and ran a hand along the pale white muslin of her sacrificial robes. She turned around and looked at the three people behind her, dressed in the same attire, hoods all down. The air was still and the low, winter sunlight shone powerfully into their eyes. Their eyes all shone right back, a ghostly yellow, somehow both absorbing yet reflecting the brightness.

The Devil's Garden was in full, deathly bloom. The discreet piles of soil that marked the shallow graves of the six child sacrifices were arranged in a circle around the four people inside it. All the surrounding trees that masked this small glade were blackened and rotted, branches hanging feebly down from some, others just gnarled stumps in the ground. There was no green grass or leafy foliage here, unlike in the deciduous forest that the rock overlooked. The soil was a brownish shade of black, filthy and infertile, hard and almost unnatural to look at. The tall man, who stood silently amongst the party snapped a black branch from one of the dying trees and used it to carve a pentagram in this soil, within the circle formed by the six graves. A single tulip sprouted suddenly from the Earth, in the centre of the circle.

"Today we will witness the Coming of the New Keeper," the old crone announced. "You are the privileged few who will bear witness." She stopped and looked at the tall man. "Thank you for coming at such short notice, Mr Taverner. Our first choice was too unreliable. We needed someone we could trust for such an important task. You are aware of your responsibilities?"

"Yes, I am."

"And they are?"

"To escort the new Keeper back to Broadoak. To ensure no harm comes to them as they will be the sole carrier of the sacred bloodline. To dispose of anyone in the Garden who becomes superfluous to the ceremony."

"This is correct."

"Thank you. This is a great honour."

"Bridget. Jennifer," the old woman said, signalling to the women. "Are you aware of your responsibilities on this great day?"

"Yes, we are," they answered in unison.

The crone approached them and kissed each of them on the forehead and smiled. "Good. The bloodline will not end here. Let us meditate on its divine evil. The ceremony will begin at twelve. All we have to do is wait."

The four of them sat in the circle and began chanting in the language of the angels.

XXXI

The small car sat parked in a lay-by, engine still running. The roads were still slightly frosty but the winter sun was shining bright in the sky, easing the temperature a little and lending the countryside vista an almost supernatural white glow. The two brothers sat inside. They had been silent for a while, each staring out the windscreen and occasionally at the clock, which now read 0845.

"This isn't how I saw my life turning out," Jeff mumbled, still staring forward.

"Oh?"

"No, it really isn't. Sat in my car, freezing my ass off, in bloody Broadoak no less, waiting for some nutter to show up and take my brother and I up to the highest point in Gloucestershire to show me the proof that black magicians killed my father."

They both laughed.

"I thought I'd be more... settled, you know?" Jeff's smile faded as he said this.

"Yeah, I thought you would be, too. Thought you and that bird would've been living in some country house with kids by now."

"That bird?"

"Natalie, was it?"

"Natasha."

"Oh yeah, that's it."

"I dunno. I guess I had it all planned at one time or another. I forget. I feel I missed a cue somewhere and messed up the whole play from that point on. Everything's gone a bit out of sync."

"I disagree. I think you've pretty much stuck to the pattern that most people do. You got drunk-k, you went out, you got laid, you took-k drugs, you had fun, you went to

157

Uni, you got a job, you got promoted, you got a flat, you made money. Now you're just in that disillusioned phase in your thirties where you miss your teens. You feel like you've already seen and done everything, so nothing has any appeal any more. Don't you ever read C-c-cosmopolitan?" He grinned.

"Can't say I do."

"You should. You'll realise you're just a regular guy."

"I guess. I suppose it all seemed more exciting when I was younger."

"You should c-count yourself luck-k-ky. I never had any of it. I sk-k-kipped straight to the disillusionment phase without doing any of the rest."

"No one's happy with their lot, I s'pose."

"I haven't been."

"What went wrong, Peter? Why did you never, well, do any of that stuff?"

"I don't know. Have you never felt like you just didn't fit in? Lik-ke you just weren't thinking, seeing, speak-k-king or feeling the same as anyone else in the room? You're almost lik-ke a ghost, just passing through them?"

Jeff grinned. "Only when I'm in the room with you."

"Exactly. I dunno. I just feel awk-kward with other people."

"I never had that. I feel fine around other people. The only thing I can't stand is my own company. When everyone else goes home, when I'm the last one in the office, when I go back to my flat, stick that stupid ready meal in the microwave, settle down to watch telly all night, that's what I can't stand. That's when I just want to crawl into a hole and die."

"So why not go out more? I don't get what's stopping you."

"No. Nor do I. I think I've just… I don't know. I feel so empty sometimes, as if I've just given up even wanting to try any more. This week's been really strange. I've actually started thinking about all this stuff for the first time, really. I think I'm going to look up Natasha when I get back to London. Just in case. You know?"

There was a pause in the conversation. Peter looked down at his lap. "I think I do. Last night, I felt something…" Peter began.

"Aw shit. Peter," warned Jeff, waving his hands dismissively. "I really don't want to know. There's a lot of things I like about you. You're my brother and, deep down, I don't think you'd ever mean to do anyone any harm. You're a good bloke. But I'm just not ready to understand that kind of shit. I don't want to hear what happened last night, ok?"

Peter paused. "I just want to be happy, you know? I'm tired of always being alone. I'm just looking for someone I c-c-can c-connect with."

"I do know." Jeff nodded and said as sincerely as he could.

"Cheers." Peter was evidently trying not to sound sarcastic. It didn't work.

The back door of the car suddenly opened and Selwyn leapt in.

"Hey boyo!" he said, tapping Jeff on the shoulder. Jeff turned around and noticed that Selwyn was wearing a fluffy white coat and a snowcap with earflaps whilst clutching a worryingly large rifle in his hands. He looked half-insane. Without the darkness of midnight to mask him, Jeff noticed just how peculiar Selwyn looked in general. He had a squashed nose, a strange overbite that accentuated his fat lips and a lock of his lank, black hair peeked through under the snowcap like a kiss curl.

"Err, Peter, this is Selwyn. Selwyn, Peter."

"Hi."

"So I take it we don't get any guns?" asked Jeff.

"Oh come on. Are you telling me that you two would honestly know how to handle a hunting rifle?"

Both brothers blushed a little. "Well, no," Jeff muttered at last.

"Exactly. So are we ready to go then, boyo?"

"Sure." Jeff pushed down the handbrake and put the car into gear as they drove out of Broadoak and towards the rock. "Why don't you tell Peter what you told me while we drive, ok?"

***

Although not too far in distance, the drive took nearly an hour through the Forest of Dean's winding, country roads. Occasionally the brightness of the winter sun was obscured entirely by the skeletal arms of trees that, at certain points on the route, completely engulfed the narrow roads, dwarfing their man-made, tarmac triviality beneath the mighty power of nature. Throughout the journey, Selwyn explained to Peter exactly what he had told Jeff the night before, but if anything with even more dramatic relish. Peter was a little dumbstruck by it and, for the last fifteen minutes or so of the ride, they all sat uncomfortably listening to the fuzzy reception on the radio as it threw choppy bursts of pop music out into the silence.

It was evident from several miles away that Symonds Yat was approaching. The rock could be seen for miles, standing over five hundred feet tall on the outskirts of the Forest. It appeared almost like a huge grey mountain, proudly towering evergreen trees and the river Severn, that was wide and magnificent this far into Gloucestershire, sparkling beneath the sun and proclaiming its dominion over the land.

"There's a car park near the bottom, we can stop there," remarked Selwyn.

"You're kidding me? You mean we have to climb that bloody thing?" Jeff replied, incredulously.

"It's hardly a climb, boyo, there's paths and everything, so there is. Think of it more just like a hike."

"Ugh. Nice weather for it."

Eventually, a small flat car park loomed at the end of a narrow dirt road and Jeff pulled over into it, parking the car and taking stock of the surroundings. There were three other cars parked there, but the remainder of the ground was empty.

"Tourists," mumbled Selwyn, nodding at the cars. "They're always coming up here. In the summer, you can't get away from them. Lots of office workers come out here for a bit of air and a go at hiking. Mind you, they soon learn that a hundred-pound pair of walking boots from Milletts won't get you far if you're used to being sat at a desk all day. There's some treacherous walks up here, so there is."

"So where exactly is this Devil's Garden then?" Peter asked, a note of impatience in his voice.

"It's up near the top of the rock."

"Don't the tourists ever find it then? It c-c-can't be that well-hidden."

"Oh, tourists frequently walk right over it. What does it matter? Everything that's suspicious about it is kept hidden well under the ground."

"What about today? You're not telling me they c-conduct these rites of theirs when there's people going up there for a hik-ke? Surely that'd be too risk-k-ky."

"Oh, no, of course not."

Peter looked expectantly at Selwyn, as if expecting him to say more. Selwyn merely tapped his nose and said, "You'll see."

"Alright, well, we'd better get going then, if you say this thing starts at midday. Lead the way."

Selwyn began to walk up a muddy path that was lined

by stinging nettles and other savage looking foliage. Jeff and Peter followed about ten metres behind, quite slowly on account of Peter's limp. When they were out of earshot, Peter whispered tensely to Jeff.

"What the fuc-k-k is he so cheery about? If what he says is true, we're all about to risk-k our bloody lives up here."

"I have no idea," replied Jeff in a low tone. "To be honest, I think he's got a bit of a screw loose."

"So why are we trusting him? This whole thing feels lik-ke a trap or something."

"I dunno. He's weird but I get the feeling he's telling the truth. I think he's just excited today because he's finally going to get his revenge or something. Either that or he just wants to shoot people."

"That's the other thing I'm worried about. What's the rifle for? Are we going to end up being accessories to murder here? I'm not going to watch him shoot someone, no matter what they're doing."

"He... I... I don't know. He seems fairly harmless. I can't picture him actually going through with anything like that."

"Maybe. But I don't trust him. Something's wrong here."

"Oh God, Peter, I know, nothing makes sense any more to me. Let's just get this over with. Whatever it turns out to be. I'm too curious. I need to know how Dad fits into all this."

"There's a point. Did you ask-k him about the letters?"

"No. Good one. Hey! Selwyn!"

The Welshman turned around, but kept trudging uphill. "What?"

"Do you know anything about letters? Like these?" Jeff pulled out one of the black letters he had taken from the Hobson' house and ran up to Selwyn.

"Oh yes. Black notes. Where did you get that?"

162

"From a friend," Jeff said, stoically.

"Oh dear, I hope they aren't *too* close a friend."

"Why?"

"A black note is a signal from the Keeper, packed with a tulip petal straight from the Devil's Garden. An order, if you like. It informs the recipient that someone close to them must be killed. It usually relates to a pact made with the Coven when you join it. If you get a black note, you know the time has come to either make the sacrifice you promised, or you die yourself."

"Oh dear God…" Jeff muttered.

"So this means the Hobsons are… in this thing too?" Peter asked, his face turning pale.

"Peter, calm down. It's probably nothing. Besides, they weren't there this morning. They'd disappeared, remember?"

"I'm worried about Sarah. What if this note was telling them to k-k-kill her?"

"Maybe they didn't want to," interjected Selwyn. "Maybe that's why they disappeared."

Peter looked at Jeff and both appeared suddenly solemn, ashen-faced.

"There's only one way to find out, isn't there?" said Peter, his eyes flashing a rare incendiary rage.

"Ok. Come on then, Selwyn. Take us up."

They continued up the hill. The weather became bitterly cold and even their heavy jackets did little to stop them shivering. The winter sun was becoming increasingly masked by thick, almost black clouds moving in from the East and the pathways that led to the top of the rock were becoming more perilous. Tiny steps made of sandstone were slippery, laced with wet mud. A couple of paths were blocked by thick undergrowth that the three of them had to fight their way through, as Selwyn insisted this was the only way to reach the Garden.

They passed a Tudor building half way up the rock that had been transformed into a pub called The Golden Lion. It looked deserted. They had not seen a single soul on the rock and all the wooden stalls that advertised cakes, biscuits and home-made teas and coffee seemed to be closed down or boarded up. It was unnerving, especially when coupled with the fluttering sounds of large birds rustling in the treetops and swooping to catch their prey from the bushes below.

As they neared the summit, the clouds grew bigger and blacker until the sky appeared dusky, even though the time was only half past eleven in the morning. All of a sudden, the clouds burst open and a torrential downpour of rain began. Jeff looked on in bemusement as, a few minutes later, a small group of twenty-somethings came running down the hill, newspapers covering their heads, shrieking to one another about how dreadful the weather was.

"You see now, how they get rid of the tourists?" Selwyn yelled to Jeff, his soaking snowcap now appeared to melt into his head like ridiculous grey, woollen mush.

"You're not telling me they c-c-control the bloody weather as well?" barked Peter, rolling his eyes and sweeping out a lock of wet blond fringe that had stuck to his nose.

"Not usually," replied the Welshman with a grin. "Just today. It's a very special day, so it is."

"Are we nearly there yet?" Jeff shot into the conversation, as he could see Peter's temper was beginning to boil.

"Funny you should ask. It's right over there." Selwyn pointed up the gravel path they were on, towards a black cluster of dead trees. They were unassuming and not particularly appealing, even less so when masked by the downpour of rain that almost concealed them. There were several trees surrounding them and, if you'd not been looking close, you would probably never have noticed anything significant about them.

They approached the black trees and Selwyn's facial features seemed to morph into something altogether more serious. His eyes became beadier as he squinted to get a better look at what was happening behind the trees. His bottom lip protruded, almost completely hiding the overbite that was usually so eye-catching. He was deep in concentration. He turned to the brothers and whispered "I think they're in there."

Selwyn, Jeff and Peter walked slowly forward, then hid behind a group of small trees that stood as close together as the men were. They craned their necks around the trees and peered into the glade protected by them. It was dry inside. The gnarled trees that hung above the small clearing were acting as a canopy against the rain. They seemed almost alive. Inside the Garden it was dark, but Jeff could make out four figures in white robes, hoods up, sat on the ground, chanting.

"Is that them?" he whispered to Selwyn.

"Oh yes."

"What are they doing?"

"They're chanting. Bringing about the start of the ceremony."

"I can't make out what they're saying."

"You won't. It's in Enochian. The language of the angels."

"What are you going to do?"

"Knock their fucking blocks off, so I am." He cocked his rifle and jumped out from behind the tree, almost farcically. The four robed figures stood up and the eldest one dropped her hood, revealing her face. Jeff saw this and suddenly leapt across the soil towards Selwyn and knocked the gun out of his hands.

"Selwyn, wait!" he yelled.

"You fool, you bloody bloody fool!" the Welshman yelled, scrambling to pick up the rifle again.

"Just wait. I know this woman. It's Ethyl Drake! She's like a grandmother to me." Jeff was smiling, full of relief that whatever Selwyn had been babbling about was obviously all harmless, if Ethyl was involved.

Ethyl smiled kindly at Jeff. "Hello Jeffrey," she said.

There was a moment's pause and before anyone had chanced to say anything else, Ethyl's eyes began to glow yellow and she stared at Selwyn. He screamed in agony, and began to convulse. Jeff stepped backwards a pace or two. Selwyn looked at him with pleading eyes, but Jeff had no idea what was happening.

"I should've realised *you* wouldn't know any better," said Ethyl to Selwyn, closing her eyes tightly. The Welshman dropped to the soil and collapsed lifeless on it, a trickle of blood beginning to ooze from his mouth.

Peter appeared behind Jeff. "What the...?"

"This... this isn't real." Jeff was still smiling, inanely. "This is, like, some kind of act. A play or something. A joke? A prank?"

Peter was shaking his head. Suddenly, Selwyn's body leapt up and grabbed Jeff by the neck, shaking him fiercely. He tried to throw him off, but the Welshman's cold hands had a tight grip on him. Peter began punching at them and trying to pry them off, all the while struggling not to look up at Selwyn's eyes, which had become blood-red orbs of rage. Giving up on niceties, Peter punched Selwyn's head hard enough for him to let go of Jeff and go tumbling to the ground.

As he hit the soil once more, he began convulsing again and two rips began to appear in his flesh, at either side of his mouth, extending up his face like a Chelsea smile. Blood streaked down his chin and cheeks as the rips grew larger and tore open his entire face, the skin peeling back like a banana, exposing the pulpy mess of veins and muscle beneath. The teeth in his mouth were chattering wildly, as his fleshless face seemed to try screaming. Blood began gushing down onto the soil and spraying up the side of Jeff's leg.

He grabbed hold of Peter's arm in sheer terror. "Run. RUN! For fuck's sake, RUN!"

The brothers both took flight and sprinted through the black trees and out of the garden, Peter ignoring the pain in his leg, too scared by what he had just seen to even care any more about anything else.

"Bring them back, Taverner," demanded Ethyl. "All of them. It is time."

The rain was coming down hard as the brothers tried in vain to find their way back down the rock. Both of them realised the important thing was to keep running, in whatever direction they could. The pair of them kept stumbling down on mud-drenched dirt paths, covering their hands, trousers and shoes with thick brown sludge.

"I've got no fucking grip on these shoes!" yelled Jeff. "Fuck!"

"Just keep running!" replied Peter, not even noticing his stutter had vanished, as they rounded a corner and came, mercifully, upon a gravel path that led down towards some hedges. The sky was pitch black now and it was becoming difficult to see, but Peter kept becoming convinced he could see a figure, or possibly figures, moving amongst the trees. Each rustling noise had his heart pounding frenziedly, whether it be a rabbit seeking shelter, a bird flying away or just the sound of his own coat catching in a bramble. The wind was howling too. Whatever had caused it, a serious storm had brewed and the noises of the rock were becoming the sounds of pure terror.

As they slipped and stumbled down past the hedgerow, a figure in black suddenly emerged before them. Jeff screamed involuntarily and grabbed a large stone from the side of the path.

"Get out of the way or so help me God, I'll fucking kill you!" he rasped, gripping the stone tightly in his hand, raising it above his shoulder.

"What?" the figure replied, in what sounded like utter disbelief.

"Jesus, Jeff. It's Sarah!" gasped Peter, as the figure came closer to reveal it was indeed Sarah Hobson, dressed in a thick black fleece jacket and a woolen ski hat.

"I knew you were coming here and I... I... just didn't want you to go and not come back," she said, still reeling from Jeff's outburst.

"How did you get here?"

"I took the bus. What's going on? Why's he going nuts?" she looked at Jeff who was looking over his shoulder and appeared on the verge of tears.

"We have to get out of here, Sarah," replied Peter, sternly, grabbing both of her arms. "You have to run, with us. We need to call the police. Selwyn's dead."

"Dead?"

"Look, there's no time. Just run! Down there!"

The three of them began to descend the slope as fast as they could when suddenly they heard the deafening roar of Selwyn's rifle firing dangerously close behind them. The smell of cordite drifted through the air, mingling with the earthy smell of the rain and the wet ground.

"SARAH! RUN!" screamed Peter, stopping in his tracks and trying to push her forward.

"Fuck off!" she shrieked back, slipping onto the ground. "I'm staying with you!"

"Stop running! All of you!" hollered a voice from further up the path. The three of them turned around to see Taverner looming behind them, barely twenty metres behind, clutching the Welshman's smoking rifle. He looked taller, wider and stronger than ever. Almost inhuman, like some kind of comic book golem.

"Taverner?" Jeff cried. "Not you too?"

"Shut it, lad. The three of you either come back up the rock with me or I'll shoot."

Peter and Jeff looked at one another. "Can we take him on? There's three of us," Peter said quietly, trying not to move his lips.

Jeff shook his head. "Take a look at us. Do you honestly think so? He's built like a brick shithouse."

"So we give up?" Sarah hissed.

"I don't know. Any better ideas? At least if we're up there, we don't know what'll happen. Down here it seems a given we're about to be shot dead."

"Alright, fine."

The three of them raised their hands in surrender and walked towards Taverner, who kept the gun firmly locked on them. "Good choice, lad," he said to Jeff, as all four of them, dripping wet, began the walk back up the muddy paths towards the Devil's Garden.

XXXII

Ethyl stood in the centre of the circle, flanked on either side by Jenny and Bridget, both of whom now stood with their hoods down. Jeff, Peter and Sarah entered the Garden again, followed by Taverner. Jeff recoiled, seeing the three robed figures stood there side by side. Old crone, woman and girl. Like the weird sisters of folklore.

"Jenny? Not you, surely? What are you doing here?" he gasped.

"Hello Jeff," she replied, coolly. "I'm here for the ceremony."

"I don't believe this. You, you told me… You fucking cried over Dad the other day! You mean to tell me you knew all along? You knew who killed him?"

"Oh please. Fuck you, Jeff. At least I managed some crocodile tears. I didn't see you shedding any at all. Don't pretend to care now."

Jeff snarled.

"Some people know too much," Ethyl interrupted.

"Secrecy is of the utmost importance to the Coven. We cannot risk being discovered. The sacred bloodline must continue. We cannot perform these rites under the petty restrictions of your weak-willed laws and we will not allow the human fleas to stop us."

"Fleas?"

"You do not understand what kind of power you are about to witness, do you Jeffrey?"

"Evidently not." He was becoming tired of riddles.

"The dark forces possess more strength than you could ever imagine, even in your wildest dreams. This whole planet is at the mercy of them. The Dark One feeds off sin and from weakness. He grows stronger with each day that passes here. Your feeble natures dispose you to sin and deficiency. Shameful lust." She looked at Peter as she said this and he bowed his head. "The Devil loves sullied flesh."

"You're insane, Ethyl," growled Peter.

"I am the Keeper of the Devil's Garden. I was born sixty-six years ago of an incestuous union. My mother and father were siblings. The Devil's black blood runs through me. It runs through all my daughters and, of course, my two beloved sons." She smiled and looked straight at Jeff and Peter.

"Sons?"

"Yes, Jeffrey. You are my sons."

Jeff began to mouth some words of shock, but no sound came out. Peter stared at Ethyl, aghast.

"Oh, I suppose I owe you both an explanation," she said, almost playfully. "I married your father in a secret ceremony, over forty years ago. We were joined in our blood. I gave him the blood of the dark one. In the orgy following the ceremony, your sister Jennifer was conceived. She was the first child to carry on the bloodline. Then in later orgies, the two of you were the fruit of our couplings. Conceived beneath the almighty pentagram. Born under the sign of the black mark. You carry the bloodline of the Devil."

"This is insane!" Peter barked. "Fucking insane!"

Sarah reached out to take his arm and implored him, with her eyes, to calm down.

"There must be many children born into the bloodline, to ensure that..." She paused. "...should any accidents happen, there will still be more who can give birth to the new Keeper, and now you are all gathered here, I'm afraid the rest of you must fall. The spare ones. The Devil sacrifices his children, just as the Christian God sent his son Jesus Christ to die on the cross."

"You're going to kill us?"

"It is necessary, Jeffrey, that you are all here, though only some of us will witness the Coming."

"How, how did you get us all here? Was Selwyn... a trap?"

Ethyl laughed mirthlessly. "No, he was just a fool. A hothead, you might say. So caught up in his own personal weakness, his lust for revenge. We knew he would bring you here. We had been planting the seeds of his vengeance for some time. Many years of careful preparation have gone into ensuring you would be here at the time of the Coming."

"How? How on Earth...?"

"You still don't understand. You think Man is so special, don't you? But you're no harder to trap than any other animal. We set a trap and we baited it, like you would for anything, from a mouse up to a deer. You all fell into it – both of you and your father too, all fell prey to what we knew would be your weakness. Whether it be lust, guilt, greed or, the lowest of them all, that most hated emotion, love. We knew it would all lead you here."

"This... this has all been some great plan?"

"Everything. From the moment your father agreed to give you over to that wretched woman whom you called 'Mummy'. We knew you would return. The only event we were not expecting was for your father to kill the little girl. We had to make provisions for an additional sacrifice. A minor disruption and one that Bridget enjoyed carrying out, thoroughly." Bridget giggled girlishly at this point.

"As for you, Sarah," Ethyl grinned, staring at the shivering young girl. "Your foolish parents were very caring. Very stupid. We wanted *you*. You had already been sworn into the Coven from birth. We owned you. But your parents wouldn't give you up. What a pity. Still, your father looked very striking on top of the bonfire last night."

Jeff swallowed hard, trying not to gag. "You mean... the... guy?"

Ethyl smiled. Sarah screamed "NO! NO! YOU FUCKING WITCH, YOU EVIL FUCKING HAG!"

Peter grabbed Sarah and tried to pull her back, stop her from running into the circle. She shrieked and cried and punched at his hands but eventually relented, collapsing into his arms as he stroked her hair and she wept into his chest.

"Don't you understand, Sarah, dear?" Ethyl's tone was patronising now. "I am no witch. This is no mere witchcraft you are dealing with. This is the ultimate evil. The very bloodline of the Devil himself. I tend the Garden here. I ensure that evil flows into the earth. That humanity is kept weak, sinful and the perfect offering. The perfect testament to the handiwork of our Dark Lord and of his Garden's Keeper. This is darkness. This is total darkness."

The rain stopped. It was not a gradual petering out. All of a sudden, the noise of the drops pounding onto the treetops and trickling down the bark came to an abrupt halt, replaced by a horrific, all-encompassing silence that felt almost deafening. The sky, just visible through the rotten trees, seemed blacker than ever and totally still.

"It is time," intoned Ethyl. Jeff glanced at his watch and discovered it was midday.

After a second or two, all three women began to chant in the language of the angels. Taverner grabbed an arm of each of the brothers and whispered harshly to them, "Stay still."

It was an eerie sight, the three women dressed entirely in white, stood side by side in the middle of the pentagram. Their eyes had rolled back into their heads and were now blank orbs, glowing ghostly yellow in the darkness created by the still, black sky and the ragged trees that hung over the assembled populace of the glade.

The chanting became faster and more furious. Jeff and Peter looked at one another. Each of them was breathing heavily and visibly. Sarah stood beside them, feeling very much detached from the proceedings but clearly afraid as she had still not let go of Peter's arm. The three robed women were now shrieking in Enochian, their hands clasped firmly to their sides, stood stock-still aside from the frantic movements of their mouths.

All of a sudden, Bridget and Jenny, with a resounding swishing sound, withdrew enormous knives from within their robes. They were slightly curved blades, almost machete-like in size and shape, but covered in arcane carvings and symbols. The symbol of the entwined silver serpents was engraved prominently on the handle of each knife.

Jeff, Peter and Sarah stepped back in terror, but Taverner pushed them back into their previous positions. "I said stay still!" he whispered again.

Before anyone could attempt any further movement, the two sisters raised their knives skywards, faced each other and, in perfect unison, brought them down again, across one another's throats, slashing with immaculate precision. Two almost graceful arcs of crimson blood jettisoned in the air, crossing one another. The blood soaked the face and hair of Ethyl, stood between her daughters, still chanting fiercely. She smiled as it ran down her face.

Bridget was the first to fall, her body collapsing in a heap at Ethyl's feet, still spurting blood from her throat all down her mother's robe and onto her sandals. Ethyl kicked at the corpse and rolled it over until it faced the brothers. Bridget's forked tongue was lolling out of her mouth, her face twisted into a sickening grin. Her eyes were blank and grey.

Jenny had her fingers stuck in her own throat wound, struggling to close it as the blood continued to stream from it, coating her hands, glazing them in red.

"Mother!" she rasped.

"Please don't fight it, Jennifer," said Ethyl, turning to her and gently lowering her hands from the throat.

Jenny, blood flowing even more freely from the wound now, dropped to the ground, falling at her mother's feet, her facial expression one of terror and despair. Jeff felt like crying as he watched his estranged sibling give up life with one last, feeble rattle from her weeping throat.

The blood from each daughter was now pouring freely into the soil. The black earth soaked it up eagerly, reminding Jeff of the ravenous way in which a pot plant drank water. There was something genuinely malevolent about this place and it sent a shiver down Jeff's spine as he fought to breathe calmly against his mounting panic.

"Blood has been spilled!" roared Ethyl. Her voice was no longer anything resembling human. It sounded like a dozen, two dozen voices all rolled into one. Many different pitches and tones. The silence surrounding them all had become a strange, unnatural roar, like being stood in the eye of a hurricane.

Ethyl reached into her robe and drew a giant sacrificial blade, like the ones her daughters had wielded. "Step into the circle, my son," she said in that ghastly spectral voice, staring straight at Peter with her glowing yellow eyes.

"Fuck you," he replied and spat on the ground.

"Do as she says," ordered Taverner, sticking the end of the rifle into the small of Peter's back.

"Fuck you too," Peter spun around. "If I'm going to die, just shoot me now. Kill me here. There's no fucking way I'm getting into that circle."

There was a pause. The stillness of the Garden seemed to grow louder, the roaring silence beginning to sound almost like a chatter of tiny voices.

"Well?" cried Peter, grabbing the end of the rifle and raising it up towards his head, staring Taverner in the eyes. "You can't, can you? You can't shoot me out here! Ha!"

Taverner looked at Ethyl questioningly.

Peter's grip tightened on the end of the rifle as he turned to Sarah. "Go on, Sarah. Run out of here. They don't want you. They want us. Run!"

Sarah looked up at Peter, her brown eyes misting with tears. "I can't leave you. What if they…?"

Peter smiled and snorted a half-laugh. "They…"

There was a tumultuous blast as Taverner squeezed the trigger of the rifle. As they looked on in mute horror, the bullet seared through Peter's jaw, shattering it in a grotesque explosion of blood, bone and teeth that showered Jeff and Sarah. The bullet flew out the back of his skull; another gushing of gore. Pieces of spattered grey matter dropped to the floor with a series of dripping, squelching noises, followed by Peter's body, the remains of his face locked in a hideous expression of surprise.

As his body fell, an eyeball, its nerves severed from the socket, plopped out and dropped onto Sarah's shoe. She screamed and erupted into a howl of frantic sobs and yelps, covering her face and falling to her knees in abject horror.

Ethyl's piercing yellow eyes focused on Peter and, in the voice that now sounded like a hundred or more voices, spoke the words, "Do not underestimate the power of evil. Do not think you can ever understand."

With that she raised her hand and Peter's corpse twitched, then sprang upwards like a rag doll on a taut string. He screamed and screamed, a ghastly wail of sheer agony. His hands slapped at what was left of his face, his fingers moving their way into the hollow socket of his lost eye and across the bloodied wall of sinew and membrane that was once his lower jaw. His tongue flopped from the bottom of his skull impotently, as he continued his incoherent shrieks.

Ethyl beckoned him into the circle and although Peter's body twitched and flailed, he was dragged in against his will by some unnatural force. The corpse finally crashed down into the soil, dead centre of the pentagram, spilling brain and blood onto Ethyl's sandals and into the anxiously awaiting thirst of the unhallowed ground itself.

Jeff was enraged beyond anything he had thought himself capable of. The shock of seeing his brother killed so brutally had triggered something and, for a second, all he could see before him was a red cloud of anger.

"And what have you got planned for me then, Ethyl?" he yelled.

"You are to help me bring about the Coming of the New Keeper," she replied.

"How? You going to kill me too?" he barked, stepping boldly into the circle and approaching her, a thread of saliva dangling from his mouth, locked in a feverish scowl.

Ethyl brandished the sacrificial blade at him. "Now, you know I cannot do that. Remember the bloodline. We here are the last of it." Her voice had returned to its normal tone now.

Jeff laughed. "So what are you saying? The Keeper has to be born of an incestuous union? You want to fuck me? Is that it?"

Ethyl grinned. "No, that isn't it. Your part to play is even more important."

"So you can't kill me?"

"No, Jeffrey. I cannot."

Jeff flung out his arm and knocked the blade from Ethyl's hand. He grabbed her by the throat and began to squeeze. "Then I'll fucking kill you," he whispered, almost spitting it into her face.

Taverner ran to the edge of the circle, cocking the rifle loudly. Ethyl shook her head and gasped "No!" at him, then turned to Jeff and smiled menacingly. Jeff screamed and moved his hand away from Ethyl's throat, instead grabbing her by the arm and dragging her to the edge of the Garden. He parted a pair of trees and dragged her through, towards a muddy precipice that marked the edge of the rock. The sky was completely black and motionless. Jeff caught out the corner his eye that his watch still read twelve, midday. The forest below was still, nothing blew the trees even though the howling sound of wind appeared to be all around. The river Severn looked stationery too.

"What is all this?" Jeff hissed. Ethyl did not respond.

He pulled her down to the ground and put his elbow against her throat, dangling her head above the edge of the precipice. He looked down past her shoulders and saw the five-hundred-foot drop towards death.

"I'll kill you. I'll fucking kill you," he whispered again.

Ethyl grinned up at him.

"I mean it. If you don't stop this, this... whatever is happening. I'll fucking kill you. There will be no Coming of a New Keeper. You said yourself, we're the last of the bloodline."

"Jeffrey, you should heed the words I said to your brother. Do not underestimate the power of evil. The trap has been set, the bait has been taken. Everything is ready. As the old Keeper, I must die regardless of anything else. You cannot threaten me with death."

"But the New Keeper can't be born yet. It must be the seed of an incestuous union!" Jeff was almost laughing maniacally as he said this, absurd as he realised he sounded.

"The seed has been planted."

"What?"

"The seed has been planted."

"Where? How?"

"Sarah is my third daughter. I gave her to those fools the Hobsons to look after until the time came when she was needed. Without even knowing, she played her part exquisitely."

"What?" Jeff was incredulous.

"You do know where your brother was last night, don't

you?" Ethyl grinned.

"I swear I'll stop you. I'll fucking stop you," he growled, staring her straight in her glowing yellow eyes.

"You are a flea, Jeffrey. Insignificant. These pathetic heroics will get you nowhere."

"No! No! GO TO HELL!" he screamed and, with an almighty shove, threw the crone off the side of the rock.

"I'll see you there!" she hissed as she toppled over the edge, head first. He stood by the precipice and watched her tumbling down the rockface. She fell straight down and appeared completely motionless in flight. He could neither see nor hear her hit the bottom. He stood up and put his head in his hands, beginning now to weep with rage and sorrow.

"Jeff…? Jeff…?" he heard a soft, broken voice saying from behind him. He turned around and saw Sarah Hobson stood there. Her face was white and her skin was cracked and scaly. Her brown eyes looked pallid and colourless. Her lips were blue. "Jeff? What's happening? What's happening to me?"

"Oh God, oh God, Sarah," he said, running to her side and reaching out for her hands. "I have no idea. I have no idea. I don't… I don't know what to do…"

She grabbed her stomach and fell to the ground once more, doubled over in pain. Jeff heard a swishing sound behind him and turned to look across the precipice, into the black sky and down into the forest. In amongst the blackness there was something moving. The howling of the motionless wind and the chattering of the voices all around made him feel like he was losing his grip on reality, a feeling made worse as he squinted and strained to make out the movement in the sky.

The black outline of a human figure appeared to be walking through the sky. It was black like nothing Jeff had seen before. Even amongst the suffocating darkness of the supernatural sky, this figure was blacker than its surroundings. It seemed to be walking in slow motion, as if on an invisible bridge between the clouds and the rock.

"The Devil!" Jeff whispered to no one, as the figure stepped closer towards him. A scream from Sarah, on the ground, made him turn back to her. She was now sprawled out, lying on her back, howling in excruciating pain. Her face was beginning to crack in places, the skin breaking and oozing blood down into her hair. Large clumps of this hair were falling out on the ground and Jeff noticed she was spitting out loose teeth and coughing up some kind of vile yellow mucus.

"Help! Help me!" she managed to gasp and Jeff knelt at her side. He motioned to hold her hand, but the skin was cracking there too, the blood and pus making it too slippery to grip. He looked down her body and saw that her stomach had swollen several times its normal size to a huge bulbous lump like an oversized watermelon. She was convulsing now, as the lump grew and her coat and shirt split wide open, exposing a torso of veiny, purple flesh.

Her hips also appeared to be expanding and it wasn't long before her trousers split, like snakeskin being shed. Her eyes had been sucked back into their sockets and now, as Jeff looked down, her face looked like a skull, hairless, eyeless and stuck fast in a muted scream. He turned around and saw the black figure from the sky was now putting its foot on the rock's surface.

Jeff stood up and began running back towards the Garden. The trees blocked his way as a cluster of thorny brambles assaulted him, tore at his skin and forced him to turn around, to take one more look at Sarah.

Her giant stomach was now thrusting upwards and she was spread-eagled on the soil. The black figure was nowhere to be seen. As Jeff watched, he saw Sarah's crotch begin to split upwards, a huge slit forming through her groin and into her stomach. Blood spilled out in what looked like pints, soaking immediately into the soil. He saw bits of intestine fall from the gap forming across her body and soon it had spread all the way to her chest, exposing her pulsating lower rib cage.

Without warning, a full-size human hand burst forth from within Sarah's innards, shaking itself free of the shiny viscera that covered it. Another hand thrust itself out and Sarah's body just collapsed back onto the ground, becoming a mangled, pulpy skin, a pile of unrecognisable bones, lurching and slithering across the soil. Something was trying to break out of this shell. A foot thrust itself out of Sarah's crotch, as a shower of uterine wall and faeces spat out onto the ground. Another followed and shortly afterwards, a fully-grown man knelt on the ground, wearing what remained of Sarah Hobson on his back like an animal skin coat.

The man stood up fully and shook himself free of Sarah's carcass, wiping bits of gore off and brushing himself down. He stood with his back to Jeff, who tried once more to run but was thwarted by the wicked brambles. The man turned around to face Jeff, slowly revealing himself. He was naked and covered entirely in the scarlet remains of Sarah Hobson. It looked almost as if his entire body was tinted red. It shone in the darkness.

Jeff stared in utter horror as he looked at the stranger's face and saw his own. The stranger smiled at him. It was his own smile he saw. In fact, the stranger's entire face, hair and body was an exact replica of Jeff's. It walked slowly, purposefully towards him, still smiling.

"Don't be afraid," the stranger said, reaching out and cupping Jeff's face in its bloodied hand. Jeff began crying. "Let me kiss you."

As the furious sound of the skies and the voices in the trees grew to an overwhelming dissonance that threatened to deafen Jeff, he closed his eyes and awaited the kiss of the stranger. Eventually he felt all-too-familiar lips pressing against his own. He could smell the blood and filth that coated this stranger. It made him feel completely disgusted, especially when the stranger thrust its vile tongue into his mouth and began licking at the roof of his mouth.

"Is it over?" Jeff whimpered, when at last the hideous thing broke free.

The stranger shook its head. "It is beginning all over again, lover."

It locked lips with Jeff once again and, with a ferocious sucking noise, swallowed him whole. The sky opened and the rain began again, pouring down with newly found fury. The stranger stood atop the rock and let the water wash over its body. The blood washed into the soil and was absorbed wholly. The cycle was complete. The New Keeper walked the Earth.

Taverner appeared from within the Garden, rifle in hand. He discarded the rifle and dropped to his knees, bowing in reverence to the stranger. "O, great lord and master, please let me serve you."

"My dear, precious servant," said the stranger. "I would like for you to take me home now."

EPILOGUE
A CRACK IN TIME

Chris Merricks' BMW crawled past the sign that read "Welcome To Broadoak – Please Drive Safely". He scowled to himself.

"These cars are meant to go bloody fast," he murmured. "Stupid country roads. Most of these fucking things aren't even on the map."

He was frustrated and annoyed. The journey from London had taken seven hours. On top of a nightmarish traffic jam on the M5, he had become severely lost in the last hour or two. Navigation was impossible on the unfathomably complicated network of lanes and B roads within the Gloucestershire countryside, only a small percentage of which actually appeared on the A – Z map he had bought at Gordano Services. As a result of overshooting far too many entrances to dirt roads hidden behind unkempt hedgerows and becoming subsequently lost, Chris was now driving at an almost unbearably slow 20mph to avoid missing anything else. He had one eye on the road and one on the map, trying desperately to reconcile the two.

At last though, he had driven past the town's welcome sign and, with relief, accelerated up to 40mph as he drove in. It didn't take him long to find the Davies Flower Shop, situated as it was on the high street, sandwiched between chemists and bookstores and other odd little shops, the contents of which he couldn't possible imagine.

"Granny's Attic?" he mumbled to himself, walking past their darkened frontages. "Merlin's Cave? Christ on a bike… What the fuck does Yer Tiz mean?"

It was now 4pm but most of the shops remained open. Certainly, the florist shop he had come to visit still had a tiny light flickering in the window, just above the hand painted 'Under New Management' sign. He shook his head in dismay at this display.

"New management, my foot. He's lost the bloody plot."

He was referring to his ex-employee, Jeff Davies with

whom he had enjoyed a close working relationship, until recently. He had known Jeff for eight years, working alongside him at HBG Telecoms in Holborn. Never once had Jeff mentioned any kind of interest in being a florist and yet, two weeks ago, Merricks had received a letter postmarked from Broadoak, announcing that Jeff would not be returning to work as planned. Instead he had resigned from his post and opened up a flower shop in his hometown, having inherited it from his recently deceased family friend, Mrs Ethyl Drake.

As Chris entered the shop, he saw Jeff stood behind the counter, looking almost identical to how he had last seen him, nearly a month ago. The only difference was that instead of wearing a sharp black suit, he was now dressed in a knitted, blue woolly jumper and a beige pair of corduroy trousers.

"Hello sir, how may I help you?" chirped Jeff, clasping his hands together in glee.

"Jeff?" Chris asked. Jeff didn't appear to recognise him. "It's me, Chris. Chris Merricks, from HBG?"

"Oh, oh my goodness Chris!" squeaked Jeff, moving out from the counter to shake the hand of his old colleague. "I'm so sorry. It's just, well, you were the last person I was expecting to see all the way up here. How's London?"

"Err, London's fine." Chris was disturbed by this uncharacteristic show of gregarious small talk. "It's the same as it was when you left, to be honest. Which is kind of what I came here to talk to you about."

"Oh?"

"Yeah, I, err, well, I just wanted to make sure that everything was ok with you, you know? I understand that you were probably upset by what happened with your… with your father…"

"Oh yes, awful business, terrible business," Jeff tutted.

"Quite. Well, anyway. I just wanted to let you know

that if you change your mind about working at HBG, then there's always a place on my team for you. You've always got a home to come back to, you know?"

"Oh, but Chris, this is my home now." Jeff spoke as if perplexed that anyone could see things any differently.

"Well, yes, but flowers? I didn't know you were into all that."

"Oh yes, I love flowers. My father's friend, Ethyl, bless her soul. She used to be forever tending to her gardens, keeping flowers and all. I remember when I used to come up as a child, she'd always show me what she was doing. I'd nearly forgotten, you know. It's amazing how we sometimes can be so absent-minded about things. We spend all our lives searching for something when it's been right there under our noses the whole time."

"You were searching for flowers?" Chris was confused and a little wary of Jeff now. He was talking like someone who had suffered a tremendous nervous breakdown.

"No, I was searching for myself. For my role in life. My place in the world, you know? I've found it here. Back home. Where I belong."

"You were doing a great job you know. At HBG. We were looking at promotion."

"I'm sorry, I'm not interested. I have my life here now."

"OK. But if you change your mind…?"

"I won't."

There was a pause.

"Jeff?"

"Yes?"

"Have you… seen a doctor lately?"

Jeff laughed. "Of course not, why would I? I feel better than I have done in years."

"I don't know, just maybe you should. You look, err, a bit peaky, not yourself, you know?"

"I think that's because you're so used to seeing old

directionless me. This is the new me, this is what I should have been all along!"

He reached out and gently tweaked Chris on the nose. Chris backed away and looked nervously at his watch.

"Well, err, I should be going. Give my regards to your family."

"Oh, there aren't any." Jeff looked away and toyed absentmindedly with a strange silver serpent ring he was wearing on his finger.

"No? I could've sworn you had a sister? And wasn't there a... brother?"

Jeff strained to think. "No, I'm sorry. I think you must have me confused with someone else. There's just me now. Now that my father's gone."

"Oh."

"Of course, we never did talk all that much did we, back in London? It must get confusing. So many people to make small talk with down there I suppose. You can never remember who has brothers and who doesn't, I imagine."

"Err, I suppose." Chris nervously played with his shirt cuffs. "Anyway, I'm sorry you've left. You were always an excellent worker and my offer still stands. If you want to come back, just give me a call. You know where I am."

He left his business card on the counter, nervously shook Jeff's hand again and made to leave the shop. Just as he was walking out of the door, Jeff called out to him. "Oh, wait!"

Chris turned around and was surprised when Jeff presented him with a single tulip. "There you go. Something for your wife!"

Chris blushed and thanked Jeff awkwardly, before bidding him farewell, leaving the shop and heading back to where he had parked his BMW. As he passed a litter bin, he discarded the flower and mumbled under his breath, "I don't even have a bloody wife. He's lost it, that one. Bloody mental."

He got back in his car and started it up, dreading the long drive back to London in the dark. An elderly couple walked past him and glanced at the vehicle and he tried his best to ignore them. This whole town gave him the creeps. Everyone seemed so nosey and into each other's affairs. How on Earth Jeff could bring himself to come live here after being in London for so long was far beyond Chris's imagination.

The pub on the corner, The Old Crown, looked so dilapidated and dark that Chris didn't even so much as contemplate stopping for a pick-me-up pint before heading off. He was far too desperate to leave. He began to drive past the river on his way out of town. The Severn looked murky and grim. The copper beech trees from the neighbouring forest swayed menacingly in the December wind. A small child on a bicycle, bundled up in what seemed like three or four layers of clothing was pedalling in circles in the middle of the road. Chris hit his horn and gestured for the child to move. A man on the side of the road shook his head and frowned at Chris, waving his hands in a "go on, get out of here" gesture. It was clear he was an outsider and not welcome here.

A small fir tree was erected in the middle of the square. Silver tinsel was wrapped around it like snakes. There were no other decorations. It looked pathetic, thought Chris to himself, remembering the grandeur of the new trees and lights that had been put up in Oxford Street earlier in the month. A mob of young carol singers stood next to the square. They stopped their singing, which didn't seem to be anything Chris recognised anyway or indeed in any discernible language, and stepped back as the BMW drove past, all staring into it to get a look at the outsider. There was something spiteful in their eyes, especially the older children. Somewhere between malice and emptiness. It crept under Chris' flesh and made him feel utterly uneasy.

He accelerated up to 40mph.

"Bloody small town mentality," he mumbled to the car radio. "How can anyone live in these shitholes? They should just bulldoze the lot of them."

He drove past a hand-painted sign by the roadside that read 'House Auction at Number 3 Monmouth Street. Furniture, bric-a-brac, clothes music cassettes! Everything must go! 15th December.'

Chris thought of his own upbringing in Vauxhall and how he'd never even had a need to see the word 'bric-a-brac' before. It was so... provincial. It almost seemed pitiably twee. He drove past the sign with no small sense of relief and back into the Forest of Dean, wondering what those sad people did with their lives all that time. How they could live, generation upon generation, trapped in such an unreal, tedious little world.

Indeed, Broadoak was his idea of Hell.

Utter Hell.

JUST BEFORE DAWN

HALLOWEEN

APRIL FOOLS DAY

LIVE FEED

MY BLOODY VALENTINE

WRONG TURN

FRIDAY THE 13TH

GOREZONE Magazine & Hadesgate Publications Present:

THE ULTIMATE SLASHER MOVIES

VOLUME ONE

The essential guide to slasher films

COMING SOON
ISBN: 978-0-9556374-0-7

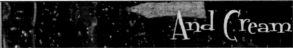

+ Bizarre Film + Cult Icons + TV Nostalgia +

Have you got the taste buds 'or the more **unusual**? Are the High Street Magazines starving you of substance, and instead forcing upon you the world of Fast Food, Gossip, Fashion and mundane Celebrity Culture? Sick of looking at Anorexic A-Listers with cellulite?

Want something more lean, tasty, and occasionally down-right bizarre?

Stop buying takeaways and feast on-line with our delectable British Baked recipe....

Serve: **Monthly**

Ingredients

2 Fluid Oz. Of **Film News**
A Pinch of **Classic TV**
Liberally added **Bizarre** Flakes for taste.
Some specially selected **Iconic Interviews** (check sell by date.)
A Sprinkle of fat Elvis Jokes......

Instructions

Just take the ingredients..... **And Cream**

WWW.ANDCREAM.COM

I scream...
You scream....
We all scream for...

And Cream